AMY REDEK

LOVE MOTEL

Hot Erotic Romance

WARNING

This book contains sexually explicit scenes and adult language. It may be considered offensive to some readers. This book is for sale to adults ONLY.

* * * * * * * * * * * * * * * * * *

Please store your files wisely where they cannot be accessed by underage readers.

Please feel free to send me an email. Just know that these emails are filtered by my publisher. Good news is always welcome.

Amy Redek - **amy_redek@awesomeauthors.org**

You might also want to check my blog for Updates and interesting info.
http://amy-redek.awesomeauthors.org/

About the Publisher

4Fun Publishing, a member of **BLVNP Incorporated**, 340 S. Lemon #6200, Walnut CA 91789, info@blvnp.com / legal@blvnp.com
NOTE: Due to the highly emotional reaction of some people to works of erotic fiction, any email sent to the above address that contains foul language or religious references is automatically deleted by our anti-spam software and will not be seen. All other communications are welcome.

DISCLAIMER

Please don't be stupid and kill yourself. This book is a work of FICTION. Do not try any new sexual practice that you find in this book. It is fiction and not to be confused with reality. Neither the author nor the publisher or its associates assume any responsibility for any loss, injury, death or legal consequences resulting from acting on the contents in this book. Every character in this book is over 18 years of age. The author's opinions are not to be construed as the opinions of the publisher. The material in this book is for entertainment purposes ONLY. Enjoy.

LOVE MOTEL

Hot Erotic Romance

By: Amy Redek

© **Amy Redek 2014**
ISBN: 978-1-62761-867-0

THOMAS LOVE was born in November, 1932, and raised in the small town of Parksville, Texas. His mother and father had been childhood sweethearts and got married in 1930, both having been raised in the same town where they now lived.

Parksville had started out as a log cabin owned by a Joshua Parks and used as a stopover for cattle drovers back in the mid nineteenth century. He supplied grog and food as well as stores to these men as they herded the cattle north to a railway depot, only because of a freak of nature the place had an artesian well that the thirsty cattle could smell for miles. These drovers usually stayed a couple of days and so in time, other cabins began to be built which finally became a small town.

The place might have grown but for the Highways Commission in their infinite wisdom, saw fit to build the north to south highway to not pass through the town but run along the outer edge on the eastern side, giving the local inhabitants just the one road branching off. From that day, the population total remained static as did business. This highway was dubbed the road from somewhere and going nowhere and most of the men now drove north to work in the city about seventy miles away.

The town boasted two churches along its wide Main Street, a school and various stores and a couple of bars. There was also a lumber mill but not big enough to use that much labour. It used to have an hotel, but with the highway now not passing through, went into decline and was finally taken over as offices for such local businesses such as a couple of lawyers, a doctor's surgery etc.

As the town expanded over the years, the streets began to parallel Main Street or bisect it at intervals and because those spreading out to the eastern side moved into a wooded area, these streets were named after trees and the outermost one where the Loves lived was called Elm Street. The bisecting roads were called Avenues and were named after past presidents, the one nearest to them was called Lincoln

Avenue and it was this one that became the town's link to the new highway and the Love's plot was three properties to the north of it.

The plots were quite large in comparison to what are offered today for it was two hundred yards on all sides, stopping about ten yards from the side of this highway. The two storied house was quite close to Elm Street, giving them a massive back garden which was mostly trees as all the others on both sides of them. In fact, this back garden was more like a wood than a garden and it gave young Tom plenty of space to play his games.

He would spend most of his spare time out there and developed the habit of wandering far afield into the other properties. Now a lot of these had not gone in for the two storey buildings but had used the ground space to make them like bungalows and had all the rooms on one level. These became the target for Tom as, as a young boy, he became a voyeur.

It was when he became tall enough to be able to see into the bedrooms of these bungalows as all of them used the back half as bedrooms and with there only being the woods at the back, seldom if ever, drew the curtains at night.

As a young man, he learned more about sex and human nature than any other person in the town. By some quirk of fate, there were no other boys of his age in Elm Street and only mixed with others when he was at school, so for the most part, he played by himself and had his adventures all alone.

Having discovered he could see all what went on in the bedrooms of the other properties, it became a regular thing for him to go to bed after dinner. Then he would then climb out of his window and clamber down the closest tree and begin his nightly forays to see what was happening in what house. He got to know all the quirks and foibles of the inhabitants as he viewed the goings on in their bedrooms.

HE WAS only nine years old when his father went off to fight the war in Europe in 1941 and was as sad as his mother when he returned in 1944 minus his left leg, having lost it in Italy. So as a growing boy, he didn't really have a father to play catch with him out in the yard or to advise him in matters of dating. So he used up his energy in the new found delight of masturbation, imitating what he'd seen through bedroom windows and almost cried with relief the first time he came. Now it was a regular habit with him to pull out his cock when watching the antics in these rooms and jerk himself off, coming all over the outside woodwork of the bungalows.

He liked the winters for it meant darkness fell earlier and he was able to start out early and not be seen as he crept from garden to garden, usually starting at the one closest to Lincoln Avenue. This was owned by Mr and Mrs Cairns. Teddy Cairns was a deputy sheriff and always seemed to be on the night shift. Now whether it was known to him or not, but Mrs Cairns, Sylvia, would quite often go down to the nearest bar of an evening and bring back another fellow to her house while her husband was out at work.

Tom would sometimes wait near the corner of the Avenue to see who she would be bringing home. She had her regulars and Tom knew them all and who was playing away from their own home. When he saw her coming, he would dart back into the trees and work his way round to the back where her bedroom was and wait.

It was invariable the same pattern she followed and he would be outside the window when the bedroom light came on and she would enter with her paramour for the night. This evening, it was Bruce Watkins, the lumber yard foreman, and as soon as they were in the room, they began kissing while he fumbled with the buttons of her blouse and kiss her throat as he struggled to get it off her shoulders. He didn't bother with unclipping her bra but just pulled it straight up so her tits fell out as he pulled it over her head and dropped it on the floor.

He kissed and sucked on her erect nipples as she crooned and stroked his head as he nibbled away while now pulling her skirt down.

Tom had seen this before and though he had his cock out in his hand, he refrained from moving for there was still more to come.

She helped Bruce get her skirt and panties off and with her naked, she kissed him as he used his fingers up between her thighs. She was by then rubbing the front of his trousers and trying to pull down the zipper as they broke apart and he took off his shirt as she succeeded in getting his trousers open and he pushed them down to let his erection spring out.

Tom marvelled at the size when he glanced down to compare the difference and couldn't wait for himself to grow up properly to have, well hope, that his cock would be just as big. Sylvia would then give it a few rubs, it looking much bigger being held in her small hand before she went down onto her knees and took the head and as much of his shaft into her mouth as she could manage. As her head began to bob on it, Tom started to work his own cock, trying to imagine that his hand was her mouth on him instead of his own hand.

But from practice, Tom only kept up a slow methodical movement of his hand and waited until she released Bruce and went and laid herself down on the bed. Her legs wide open for him to see the folds of her sex and the shining wetness of her juices as Bruce climbed on the bed, his cock swaying and bobbing about as he moved between her legs. He watched that massive cock disappear up into her and he heard the grunts they both gave out as their bodies met and watched as Bruce began to fuck her.

Now Tom started to move in time to Bruce, copying the forward thrusts on his own cock though he was drawing back his foreskin as Bruce fucked Sylvia. He knew from seeing them before when Bruce was reaching his peak for the arse facing him was now moving faster and the grunting was turning into pants as he ground himself harder into her and Tom followed as Bruce cried out in his release. Tom had to remain mute as his sperm began to splatter the wall outside as Bruce sent his up into the woman beneath him.

Even though Tom had now had his release, he still stayed to watch Bruce pull out, his prick still up hard but now shiny and wet from his coming and her juices. Sylvia was then quickly up onto her knees to suck on his wet and still throbbing cock.

Tom chuckled to himself as he put his wilting cock away that he knew something that she didn't and that was only five houses down, in about an hour's time, her husband would be fucking Mrs Kleinsman. Only with a difference, for she liked being fucked up the arse. Tom knew that in an hour he would be ready to do it again and so he made his way down there to wait and dream of what it would be like to actually put his own cock inside a woman.

Tom had sat down with his back to a tree to wait for the bedroom light to come on in Widow Kleinsman's house. That she was a widow was a bonus for Teddy Cairns as he knew there wouldn't be any interruptions or comebacks. She was kinky in the fact that she always met Teddy wearing her late husband's clothes and because she acted the part of being a male, insisted on having her sex in this way. Though she never took her trousers off and only dropped them down round her ankles before bending over the chair in her room and having him fuck her up the arse.

He used a condom for this, which made sense, and seemed to revel in the tightness of her as he told her. All their words coming out quite clearly to Tom outside as he watched and jerked himself off in time again to Teddy's movements, coming at the same time. She too seemed to copy Sylvia in when he'd finished coming, pulled off the condom with some tissues and then knelt down and sucked him off.

It was something that Tom had never seen Sylvia do to her husband in all the times he'd seen them have sex. She went down on all her other men friends but he'd never witnessed her do the same for her husband. Strange how women think, he thought.

THERE ARE three others that Tom viewed though we can bypass the Costellos for they only seemed to perform the sexual act between themselves once a week and underneath the bedclothes, much to Tom's annoyance. We will come to the other two later for there is a bit more history to come that relates to Tom and that is of his aunt.

She was the elder sister of his mother and owned an hotel up in the city, right next to the railway station. A rundown place that saw its heyday at the turn of the century when the cattle still came to the railroad for onward shipment to the north. Aunt Edith Konisberg, like his mother, was of Danish origin, but had never married, even on inheriting the hotel outright with Tom's mother having got married. She'd had many suitors, especially when it was known that she had become the owner of the Railway Hotel, but never took to any of them.

Not ever trusting any of her staff, she never took time off or holidays and therefore, the only time she saw her sister or nephew was when they visited her, which wasn't very often for, dilapidated though the hotel was, it was nearly always full so they very seldom got together. With Tom it was different, for there was a little box room next to the bathroom on the first floor landing that he didn't mind sleeping in. It gave him a chance to be away from home and explore the city.

His aunt always welcomed and even pampered him to the point that he could come and go as he pleased and was never told when it was time for bed. It was also the place where he first ever got drunk, after having stolen a bottle of gin from the bar which turned him off of drink because of the way he felt the following day. As mentioned, his room was really only used for storage and only had room for a camp bed and for his clothes, he had to use nails instead of proper hooks in the walls.

It was on one particular day when he was staying there that he tried to add an extra nail and found that after just one blow, it had gone right through the thin partition. On looking at what he had been hanging some of clothes on, were in fact, the ends of screws that had come through from the bathroom.

He went round and checked and found that these screws were holding up a cabinet above the basin and faced the toilet seat, the bath being off to the left as you faced the mirror which was attached to the door of said cabinet. Being the voyeur he was, saw the possibilities of this cabinet and so went and found a screwdriver and, with some difficulty because of the layers of paint over the years, finally was able to remove this right hand lower screw.

He went back into his box room and saw that he had a perfect view of the toilet through the screw hole though he found it of no use when a man used the pan for a piss. He got to see a lot of women drop their knickers and have their pee and wipe themselves, but to him it wasn't enough and so the next time the toilet was vacant, he went and tried to take out the other bottom screw that was closer to the bath but couldn't shift it, so he took out the top one. He'd seen some women taken their clothes off but always missed the bit of seeing them completely naked as they got into the bath. He found he had to stand on a box to see through this one, with his face pressed to the wall, but he still couldn't see all that he wanted to.

Then one day he saw this pretty thing go into the bathroom with a towel draped over her arm but after climbing onto the box and trying to swivel his eye through this small hole couldn't see more than the hair on her head as she undressed for her bath.

There was only one answer to this and the next day he borrowed a pair of pliers and worked at the end of this bottom screw and managed to free the other end from the paintwork that had prevented him earlier from removing it. Round to the bathroom he went and with the same pliers, was able to twist the screw and finally get it out.

He went back to his box room to check on what the new hole gave in the viewing of the bathroom when he heard someone enter on the other side. He couldn't see who it was because the new hole was still partially blocked and he only had the view of the opposite wall when looking through the top hole. So with a nail taken from one of the other walls in his room, he poked it through and cleared the blockage and found that he could see far more than before.

He now saw that the occupant of the bathroom was an old dowager duchess who was a friend of his aunt and what a revolting sight she was. She was at least sixty if she was a day. Her hair, or what was left of it, was pushed up into an old mop cap and her shoulders were scrawny as were the obscene things hanging down her chest that once had been tits. In comparison to the Cinderella that he wanted to see, he was now looking through this fresh hole at the wicked witch.

Now when he had used the nail to enlarge the hole from the room he was in, he'd also moved the cabinet, breaking the paint seal that had helped to keep it fixed to the wall. Without this extra adherence, the weight of the cabinet proved too much for the one remaining screw to hold it. The cabinet suddenly parted company with the paintwork and wall and fell into the bathroom with a fearful crash. The ancient crone inside screamed with fright and Tom fell off his box with shock, and dived out of his room as fast as he could go. He missed his footing at the top of the stairs and tumbled down head over heels the whole length.

Tom remembered seeing the old woman come storming out of the bathroom, a towel partly draped around her. One floppy tit exposed and flapping about as she waved her arm screaming the vilest of names at him that she could only have learnt in an army barracks. He couldn't help but laugh as he lay in a heap at the bottom of the stairs, even though he was in pain from a broken collar bone and two broken wrists.

His aunt managed to quieten down the old bitch and get her covered up and back into the bathroom before she attended to him, that in the end, turned out to be to his advantage. He was duly patched up in splints and plaster and installed in his bed in the box room he'd been allocated. It was almost a month before he had the plaster casts removed and returned to his own home.

It was Tom's last holiday in the hotel for his aunt died the following year and left the hotel to his mother and father. But as they had no intention of running the place, sold it and put the money it fetched into the bank for Tom's further education after his tour of military service.

Tom kept up his nocturnal visits to neighbouring houses to look into their bedrooms at night and it is now time to relate the other two that were on his row. The Yates were an ordinary couple though she turned a bit funny after her husband died in a road accident a few years later so we'll come back to her quirky nature after this event.

So he went to where the Robinsons lived. They were an elderly couple who had the misfortune to be both deaf and dumb. In spite of their own physical defects, were able to produce a normal son in respect of hearing and speech. Though not normal in the accepted sense of the word for he was somewhat on the effeminate side, though even that is wrong because half of his wardrobe consisted of the attire of a sweet young female.

His name was David and a slim gangling youth who didn't go out a lot, and much to his parents' delight, was glad that he had a friend in Bert Jones who would drop in once a week to talk to him and listen to records. What they didn't know was that he stayed the night and didn't leave till after five in the morning.

Having passed other houses going through their back gardens, he arrived at David's house and saw that the curtains to his room hadn't been drawn and that David was lying on his bed reading a magazine. So it was a matter of Tom waiting to see if he had been correct in the pattern of Bert in his visitation times to see David.

He didn't have to wait long before he saw the bedroom door open and Bert walk in carrying a six pack of beer.

'Hello, darling. You're so late,' cried David, throwing the magazine to one side as he jumped off the bed to fling his arms around Bert's neck and give him a kiss on the lips. 'I didn't think you were coming tonight but I still made some little cakes for us to eat, on the side there. Put the beers down and you can watch me as I change.'

Bert sat down heavily in the only chair that the room provided and popped open a can of beer and watched David as he pirouetted across the room to his wardrobe. With the wardrobe door open, the mirror attached to the inside, gave Bert and Tom, a two dimensional view of this slim boy. His hair was a little longer than a crew cut and carefully swept back to show off his small ears. His face was narrow and his nose small, but he had wide big eyes and lashes that any girl would have been desperately envious of.

He quickly pulled off the shirt that had been knotted at the front and threw it into the open wardrobe, the thin gold chain about his neck glinted with reflected light as it swung about. His thin chest was devoid of hair as were his legs as he shucked off his jeans. His shorts quickly followed and naked, turned to the mirror and went up onto his toes, slowly swaying from side to side as he looked at his reflection.

'Mirror, mirror on the wall,' David started to quote causing Bert to snort and splutter beer down his front. 'Well I am!' David retorted, swinging round to face him, hands on hips.

'Get on with it,' Bert said, wiping his mouth with the back of his hand. David gave him a finger and turned back to the wardrobe and pulled out a small wispy piece of material which turned out to be panties. He put these on, tucking his small penis inside and gently smoothing down the front to make it as flat as possible. Then he pulled out a small padded bra which he slipped on and expertly clipped it up at the back. A suspender belt was deftly fixed round his waist and sitting down on a small stool, quickly pulled on stockings and clipped them to the belt. As he stretched his legs in turn to smooth out the silk, he had a small smile on his face as he looked at Bert's reflection in this wardrobe mirror. David could see that Bert was getting excited by the colour slowly rising to his face and noting the bulge at the front of his trousers.

Turning on the stool to the desk which served as a dressing table, he opened a drawer and pulled out a small compact and dusted his face lightly and flicked some powder down his arms. Next he brought out some lipstick and this was gently applied to the top lip first and then the bottom one before he pressed the two together and then lightly dabbed them with a tissue. He was then up again to the wardrobe and pulled out a summer frock which he quickly slipped over his head and smoothed it down over his hips before he lightly tripped over to Bert.

'Zip me up, darling,' turning round and Bert put down his beer and pulled up the zipper at the back of the frock but then grasped David's arm, who gave out a laugh and twisted away, making the hem of the frock swirl out, giving Bert a sight of white thighs above the black stockings held up by the suspender straps.

'Am I pretty? Am I still your pretty little girl?' David asked coyly. Bert nodded dumbly and held out his hand.

Tom outside of the window also nodded as though the question had been asked of him. He was amazed at the transformation that had taken place, enough for his own prick to rise hard inside his trousers. He fumbled with the zipper and finally released his erection to be ready when the action started.

David went over and sat down on Bert's lap and gave him a slow, sensuous kiss as Bert's hand stroked the silken clad thigh. David held Bert's head as he bent and nibbled and kissed his neck and shoulder.

'Oh darling, darling. It's been a whole week since I've seen you. I do love you so, I do,' David whispered as he started to un-button Bert's shirt, nibbling at his ear as he tried to get it off of Bert's big shoulders. Sliding off his lap, he got the shirt off and undid the belt to his trousers and pulled at the waist band. Bert lifted himself up to assist and let them slide down with his shorts, his erection springing free. Long, pale and slender, the circumcised prick stood out red headed from his sparse bush.

David took it gently between two fingers and started moving the outer flesh up and down the muscle that was sheathed by this soft outer skin. Twisting and bending his head low, he took the pair of balls into his mouth and gently moved them about with his tongue. Bert eased himself to be more comfortable in the chair and picked up his can of beer and sipped at it as he watched David work on him. The red lips and pink tongue moving up and down his shaft, nibbling and sucking at him, finally taking the purpling head into his mouth causing Bert to groan with pleasure.

David's head now started moving faster up and down, bringing more groans from Bert as his body tensed up, his hips starting to buck as he came. Keeping his head moving, David took the hot stream into his mouth as Bert bucked beneath him, giving him all that he had inside his balls. David's face was flushed and his eyes sparkling as he lifted his head up off the red swollen gland and nuzzled it to his cheek. He opened his mouth to let Bert see what had come out of his prick before swallowing it all.

'That was beautiful, Bert darling,' he sighed, looking up at him as he held the still throbbing member to his face. He then got up from the floor and peeled Bert's trousers off from round his ankles and threw then onto the bed. He picked up his own dressing gown and draped it across Bert's knees and settled down in his lap, tenderly putting his arm round his neck, taking hold of the beer can and having a sip before handing it back.

Tom had liked the dressing up show of the transvestite David, but had been disappointed in what he had seen of the action. He was about to leave when David jumped up off of Bert's lap.

'I've learnt a new dance, darling. Wait till you see it,' and went to his record player and put on a medium fast record, and as the music played, he swirled around in time to the music and slowly began to peel off his frock.

Tom stayed to watch as it might be as good as the dressing part. But it was only the frock that came off. David doing his dance in the bra, panties, suspender belt and stockings, but it was the sexiest dance Tom had ever seen a boy do. Bert obviously thought so too, because David suddenly whipped the dressing gown away from Bert's lap to reveal him with another hard on, upright and swaying from the gown's withdrawal movements.

David grabbed Bert's hand and pulled him up from the chair and led him over to the bed. Bert sat down as David went to his dressing desk and coyly slipped off his panties to reveal the pale white cheeks of his bum. Then with one finger, dipped it into a pot of cream and in one quick swift movement, smeared it round his back passage. He quickly crossed the room and lay down on his back on the bed, and as he did so, he pushed his own small cock back between his legs so that he lay there like a young woman readying for fucking.

Bert turned and rolled over and lay on top of David and started to kiss him. The arms came up and went round his head and returned the kisses with passion. It was Bert who broke off, rolling back onto the bed.

'Roll over,' he growled.

David smiled up at him and obediently rolled over onto his stomach. Bert rose up and moved in between David's legs and grasped his hips and pulled him up into a kneeling position. He could now see the cream covered orifice surrounded by the suspender belt and stockings that seemed to increase his excitement.

He held his stiff prick in his hand and nuzzled it into the cream, smearing the head of it as he slowly pushed himself into the boy. Taking a firm grip of the hips, pushed himself further forward and slid completely in up to the hilt till he was fully embedded inside. Bert's head went back as he gave a little grind to David's backside before he started to move himself in and out of him. They were savage short sharp thrusts as he fucked David who groaned and squirmed under the onslaught. Faster and faster Bert moved till he gave out a groan and changed from thrusts to jerks as he came inside the boy, collapsing on top of him and both fell flat to the bed.

That's more like it, thought Tom as he came too, splattering the wall and flicking the drops off the end of himself before putting it away. Not bad, but almost the same sequence that he last saw not too long ago, but still wondered why Bert should go fucking a boy when he had that beautiful wife at home ready for it at any time.

TIMES WERE hard for Tom and his family what with his father now being disabled from losing his leg during the war and not being able to work and became more disgruntled that his wife had to go back to work to help supplement his paltry pension. She had once been a teacher at the local school to which she now returned though they could have used the money that was the result of her sister's death and the sale of the hotel, but that they were determined to save for Tom's further education. In consequence, it was one of the reasons that Tom spent more time at home instead of mixing with his peers and so had developed into a rather shy boy in company and if it hadn't been for Caroline, he would never had have the courage to ever approach any of the local girls for the purpose of sex, hence his predilection for watching other people's sexual activities. Most of his time at the weekends and early evenings were spent with his father to keep him abreast of what was happening in the town.

Then Tom received his papers for him to go into the army. His mother burst into tears the day they arrived, knowing that it was inevitable, but cried all the same.

Distance, like time, is relative. He knew how far it had been to go to school and how long it would take him. He was therefore surprised that it took him nearly two days to report for military duty and he was still in his own country. He'd only ever been as far as the city which was only seventy miles away, but now he had to travel over a thousand.

He had said a loving goodbye to his ageing parents at the bus depot and within two months, was back again on compassionate leave. It had never been ascertained exactly how the fire had started in Elm Street, but it swept from north to south at an alarming speed. It only took the houses on the east side, moving rapidly through the trees and houses in its path till it was halted at Lincoln Avenue. This thoroughfare that was the link between the town and the highway. The local firemen knew they had no chance to save the houses because of the density of the trees in the gardens of the houses in the path of the fire and so concentrated their main fire tenders in Lincoln Avenue to prevent the fire from jumping across. This they managed with the two tenders they had and so stopped it from spreading further, but eight houses had been lost in the path of the fire, Tom's being one of them

All other occupants of the houses consumed by the conflagration escaped except for Tom's parents. With their bodies being found on the ground floor, the fire having happened during the night, that due to his father's disability, they'd only managed to get down the stairs before being overcome by smoke, basing this theory on the coroner's inquest after the autopsy. Smoke inhalation was attributed to their death and that they had actually died before they were burnt.

Tom was grief stricken when he was told the news by the commander of the training post and he was given his leave to attend the funeral. This again was a two-day journey south and he looked with anguish at seeing the still smouldering remains of the trees that lined the highway among which was the remains of his house before the bus he was on turned into Lincoln Avenue to drop him off at the bus depot in town.

In such a small town, everybody knew most of everybody's business and it was the bank manager who assured the funeral parlour that there was enough money in their account that would now belong to Tom, to pay for the funeral, and so knowing when Tom would arrive, the funeral had been arranged for that day.

So two hours after arriving in the town, he was there at the church for the service to his dead parents and went with a surprising number of townspeople to see to their burial.

Tom had had two days to get over the shock of never seeing them again and so was able to talk to the pastor and the bank manager who had also attended and see to the payment exacted to see his parents buried. He was also assured by said bank manager that their wills and insurance papers had been lodged with the bank and so he wouldn't be short of any monies in the future. But at the time, this went un-noticed by Tom and knowing he still had two hours to wait for the bus that would pass through town again, spent the time walking through what had been his garden to see the still smoking ruin of what had been his home, now reduced to ashes, only half of the chimney stack still standing and only then did he cry alone there.

With the town not having an hotel and not accepting the several offers he had to stay the night, caught the bus back to the town and stayed for the night at the hotel that had once belonged to his aunt. This time as a paying guest.

He then returned to his training unit to finally be passed out as a marine and was soon shipped out to fight in Korea.

For nearly two years, he spent more time digging foxholes and vowed that when he got home he would never ever lift another shovel of dirt. He fought too and in that time was wounded, minor though which gave him a few weeks respite from the rigours of the winters that froze as many as were killed by actual combat. But he survived to the cease fire and was glad to be amongst one of the first battalions to be sent back home.

One of the memories he took back with him apart from the sweating heat and the freezing winter was the time in Seoul when recuperating from his wound. A couple of the men went along to a whorehouse and being his usual shy self, declined to actually go with one of the many women offered. The madam of the house then suggested if he would like to watch others having sex. Now this was much more appealing to him and so he said that he would like that, though it still cost him as much as if he'd gone with one of the women.

He was taken up a narrow staircase and into a tight and claustrophobic corridor that had several curtains along one wall. The girl who was leading him, stopped at the first one and drew the curtain back and he found that he was looking into one of the bedrooms of the house through a one sided mirror. This was more to his liking to watch two couples have sex on the bed below him and got an instant erection.

He was dragged along to the next window to see one of his friends taking a young Korean up the backside and got a vicarious thrill as he thought of Bert and David and was now really throbbing inside his trousers and had just got his cock out of his trousers when he was pulled along to the next window to see another young girl, this time taking his sergeant's cock into her mouth. He now began to jerk himself off but the girl who was showing him these scenes pulled his hand away and began to do it herself and went down onto her knees and took him into her mouth and sucked and tongued him as he watched through this window and came about the same time as his sergeant, but his girl took it all in whereas the sergeant sprayed all of his coming over the girl's face and laughed as she tried to catch the flying sperm with her open mouth.

Tom went back quite a few times, being the voyeur and having himself jerked off or taken in the mouth by the girl he was with as he watched the antics of the others in their own forms of sex. These forays into Seoul had a lasting effect on Tom and he formulated an idea of doing something of this nature when he returned to the States but for his own pleasure as a voyeur.

He was duly sent back and eventually demobbed, using the English term, and collected his final pay which was more than enough for him to buy a camper van. He'd learned to drive while in the army and now had a licence to this effect. Plus he didn't have a home as such to go back to so he had to have somewhere to sleep and this fitted in with the plans he had formulated in his mind.

He took his time driving south for he stopped at quite a few motels to see how they were run, and here he crossed his fingers, that nobody had thought of doing this at his town for that was what he wanted to build and open. A motel! Love Motel he was going to call it using his own name but also give it the atmosphere where people could also go to make love as well as sleep. He was going to make it into a voyeur's dream and so he hoped and prayed that a motel had not been opened before he'd got there.

So it was with some trepidation that after having passed through the city and passed the sign that told you that it was only five miles to Parksville that he began to worry. He was still a mile away when he could see an illuminated sign and he thought his hopes had been dashed but was relieved when he recognised that of it being one of a petrol company.

Nature had taken its course and there was now quite an abundance of new growth that had started to cover the scene of the fire that had killed his parents and made others homeless and came close to Lincoln Avenue to find that the corner plot that once had belonged to Deputy Sheriff Cairns was now a service station. One that also had the garish sign denoting that it had a diner as well.

He turned off into the avenue and went down and cruised along Elm Street and noted that only one house had been rebuilt since the fire and that was the place that belonged to the widow Yates, three along from where his house had stood. This boosted up his hopes in his future plans for his own property. He drove back along the street and pulled into what was his own ground and parked near the now, weed overgrown ruins of what had been his home.

His camper van by modern day standards was small, but for him then, it was big enough to have a lounge and separate bedroom as well as a shower and toilet closet. All small but just big enough for one. Here he spent his first night back and cried for the loss of his parents.

On his journey down with the hope that nobody else had built a motel, he'd made drawings, and these he gathered together the next morning after breakfast. As glad as he'd been to get out of uniform, having been made up to sergeant, he donned it once again along with his ribbons, went to the town hall, emphasising a limp as a war wound, to present his request for planning permission to convert his property into a motel, opening out onto the highway.

He was greeted as a war hero with his purple heart and other decorations and his application was passed through immediately and by the end of the day, he had the blessings of the town in his project.

What with the house insurance from the fire, his parents separate life insurance policies as well as what was left from his aunt, he was well found for funds. So to celebrate, if you could call it that, he had dinner at the petrol station's diner instead of cooking it himself.

Next day he began the work to change his former home and land into a motel. First was to seek out the Costellos whose property lay between him and the petrol station and found that they had, instead of waiting for their house to be rebuilt, had bought another property on the other side of town and were only too happy to sell him their original piece of land. Okay, it would take a day or two to get it on paper but it was enough for him to start work.

He spoke to a contractor saying that he wanted him to clear the two properties of the debris of the houses from the fire as well as clear a good amount of the new growth from the land that faced the highway. They agreed on the price for the man knew exactly where Tom had lived and said that he would be along the following day with a digger and a truck to take away what was cleared. Tom was fractious at night now for he didn't dare go over to the far side of Elm Street to peer through bedroom windows as he wasn't too sure of the lie of the land over on that side so had to content himself with just masturbation while looking at some of the books he'd picked up in Korea. Not only did he have these books but he also had a letter that he'd received from Caroline just before he'd gone into the military and it now helped him through this period. He'd just turned eighteen which made her around twenty one.

She'd started off the letter by reminding him of fact that it had been her aunt that he had seen in the bathroom of the hotel and had sat with him on several times to read a story to him. "Well, it was not long after this that we left England."

Tom then remembered that the letter had a foreign stamp on the envelope but couldn't think of what country it had been from.

"We went by boat," the letter continued, "and I got to know a lot of how ships are run. Mostly by fornication. That's the genteel way of saying fucking. They were a randy lot from the captain down and the language of the seamen wasn't fit for the ears of the niece of a Duchess. I'll save the story of that ship for another letter except I must tell you this bit. Did you know that wireless operators are picked for the speed at which they can send out messages by the telegraph key? They're fantastic! One tapped out the whole of the national anthem on the bud of my clitoris in two minutes while I played on his horn pipe. It was great!

"Well, anyway, we finally got there. (She never did say where but Tom came to the conclusion by the rest of the letter that she meant India.) We landed and were herded aboard a train and had a horrible journey inland. It was hot! It stank, and the bloody flies, well! Millions of them! There must have been one fly for every black and I think they all tried to board the train at the same time. The flies I mean. I wore as little clothing as I could though this didn't mean leaving much off with my aunt the Duchess around. But still, with the heat, I couldn't wear any undies, which meant I then started to get flies coming up under my skirt. Bloody things, they must have been male flies and they drove me mad. I was damn glad when we finally got off of that train.

"But that was only to transfer to a carriage drawn by what looked like the candidate for the next day's cooking pot. We were carried to some palace or other, a big sprawling place that was full of carvings and such like. Lots of servants about wearing white smock like jackets that came down to their knees, below which they had baggy white trousers and funny looking towels round their heads which I knew to be called turbans.

"Mind you, they were very polite, always putting their hands up together before them as if in prayer before bowing their heads every time you spoke to them. I don't think there was a real man amongst them! I was really itching for one, especially after all those flies trying to have sex with me under my skirt. My brother hadn't come with us for he had been left behind in England and I wondered what he was doing for sex?

"Well I was treated like a queen in this palace of the Rajah, or whatever he was, and me being there without a consort. There were so many servants about the place at all times that I couldn't even play with myself. A female servant even had a cot in my room with just a gauzy thing draped down to curtain her alcove off from my room space. When in bed, I only had to move slightly and she was there asking if I was uncomfortable or not and if there was anything she could get me? I felt like screaming that I wanted a big fucking cock! I was getting really desperate.

"There was only one place I found that I could touch myself without them knowing and that was in the bath. Though this was a bath that you'd never imagine for it was a huge sunken thing in a room all of its own. There in the middle, all tiled and filled with lots of hot water and all kinds of bottles of scents and perfumes along the sides. The girls would undress me and I would walk down these steps, yes, steps, into this hot scented water and settle myself down with the water covering my shoulders.

I managed to knock one of these bottle off the edge into the water and hide it in my hand and while they let me soak for awhile, I would use this bottle, ramming it up into myself trying to imagine that it was some big cock that was fucking me but it wasn't any use. The place, the constant attendants, the furtiveness of it all made it impossible for me to come, let alone get excited under these conditions.

"Then after my soaking, two girls would get into this huge bath as well and begin to wash me. After this, I would be helped to stand by this pool, well it was big enough to swim in, and they would dry me with big massive towels. Then I would lie down on a table and have oils and scents rubbed into my body. This excited me when they rubbed my tits and the insides of my thighs but I still didn't get any relief. At least Mafeking got relieved but not me.

"Well I did eventually.

"The colonel of the garrison nearby sometimes visited the palace and I overheard that their annual regimental dinner was soon and he invited the Rajah, or whatever he was, to attend with his guests. My aunt, the Duchess, started to make her apologies but I jumped in quick and thanked the colonel very much and said that we would be delighted to come. I was going to come one way or another. Aunt protested but she got over-ruled for a change and soon the big night came. Was or was I not excited? I hadn't had a man for weeks let alone see a real one in the flesh for the same period of time.

"It was a Scot's regiment and in spite of the heat, were still wearing full regimental mess kit. They must have been bloody uncomfortable in that humid atmosphere in spite of the ceiling fans being wafted backwards and forwards overhead. I put on the lowest neckline dress that I had and that was all, apart from my shoes. The evening was hot and in spite of this, I put on a shawl to cover my bare shoulders and also so that my aunt couldn't see just how low the neckline was and at how much tit I was showing. I took the shawl off when we arrived but it was then too late for her to say or do anything about it. I knew I would get it in the neck later when we would return to our apartment, but I didn't care for there were men there.

"There must have been at least fifteen other women there, wives and what have you but I know that I was the prettiest. Aunt and I were escorted into a large room where everybody was gathering together for drinks before dinner would be announced. You could hear the gasps from these women when my low cut dress was seen as the air suddenly became electrified.

"I became a magnet but one with two different poles. One attracting the men and the other repelled the women. I could see the women's heads getting together whilst looking at me knowing that it was I that was being discussed. There must have been around forty officers in that room and the whole time I was in there, I must have had at least half of them around all that time. My glass wasn't allowed to stay empty, and the questions! Heavens above! They never stopped coming and though some of them were suggestive, I couldn't really reply or take them up.

"The room, when I got a chance to look around, was quite colourful. The regimental battle flags were draped all over the walls, the men in their bright coloured jackets above their tartan kilts. It was a shock at first to see men dressed like this and showing off their knees but after several minutes it looked almost natural and went with the atmosphere of the place.

"Somebody must have given out a signal that dinner was ready because everybody suddenly started shuffling about and ladies were being collected from their chairs around the walls. A red faced man stamped to attention in front of me, really startling me and stammered out that he was to be my escort into dinner. Captain something or another for I didn't quite catch it with his accent as he bowed first and then offered me his arm. It was so old fashioned that I nearly laughed but I played the game and I curtsied deeply, staying down longer than is proper so that he got a bloody good eyeful of my tits nearly falling out over his boots. I came up with a smile on my face and you should have seen his! I nearly spoilt it by laughing. It was redder than his tunic and I don't think he'd seen a proper woman for years. I had moved forward slightly when I came up from my curtsey for my tits were then almost under his nose as I turned and took his arm to let him lead me into dinner.

"It was a sumptuous feast and I don't think I could put a name to any of the dishes that were served up. But before this, we were seated and a piper came in and paraded round the massively long table leading two waiters bearing a loaded tray that was eventually placed up near the top. Then everybody got stuck in to eat and all the time we were stuffing ourselves, two poor sods in that heat had to keep playing on their pipes. Funnily enough, it didn't sound so bad for I normally can't stand the wailing of them.

"I was sat quite a way down the table for I was really a nobody. The Rajah, or whatever his name was, was at the top, the Duchess, my aunt, quite close to where he sat. Some old bag was on the other side of the captain that escorted me and was sitting on my right and I had a young subaltern seated to my left. I played the very devil with that young lad. In fact I had both of them in one hell of a state before dinner was halfway through, rubbing my legs against theirs etc.

"The captain almost jumped out of his skin when I slid my hand into his lap and touched his cock. I'd put my hand under his kilt and sporran, you know, that funny furry lap bag they wear. Then I drew his hand to put it on the inside of my thigh. He had a problem eating as I held it there trapped between my legs. The young lad on my left would be telling his story for years I should think. I'd put my hand on his knee and slowly dragged my fingertips up his leg till his kilt was bunched up at his lap. His face was red as he reached out and clutched his wine glass.

"I waited until he had a mouthful and then grabbed his prick! They don't wear anything under their kilts, well, not in that hot weather anyway. I grabbed his cock which was standing up to the salute and he choked on his wine as I expected. He spluttered it everywhere and tried to wipe his mouth with a napkin as he apologised to those at the table. There were smirks on the faces of the other officers having guessed by looking at my innocent face of what had happened beneath the table. The subaltern's face must have shown it as well, for, even though it was hot in the room, his face was pouring with sweat as I played with his cock. He wiped his face with his napkin, but the sweat continued to break out on his forehead and another officer passed him a clean one saying it looked as if he needed some relief. This lower end of the table which was nearly all men, exploded into laughter which caused the heads of those at the other end of the table to look down at us.

"I brought his ordeal to an end by working my hand furiously till I felt the throbbing spasms as he shot his load out under the table. I passed him my napkin which he dabbed his lips with it first before whipping it down below the top of the table.

"Thank you, he said, looking at me for the first time since I'd taken him in hand. My pleasure, I replied, giving him a sweet smile.

"Dinner came to an end and we were treated to another round the table trip by the pipers before we were led back out into that other hall for some more drinks, though these being a bit more on the stronger side.

A space was cleared in the center of the floor and we were treated to a display of their sword dance or whatever it's called. You know, where they put down two swords crossed and then dance on almost tip toes between the blades. Stepping lightly over them and moving up and down in little hops. The dance I wanted was on a bed where the man moved in and out.

"Drinks were going down fast and the party started getting rougher and some of the officers were now passing out. Standing there one minute and then keeling over the next, out cold onto the floor. There were cheers at this and some of them would grab the poor unfortunate by the heels and drag him away. Where they dumped them, I don't know.

"Then I spied my aunt giving out her goodbye speech and as I've seen it so often I was able to recognise it from the other end of the hall. Christ, I said to the captain, she's going already and the party's only just beginning. Get me out of here and tell her that I was feeling unwell and have already been taken home. He rapped out an order to someone and a small crowd of them hustled me out of sight into another room off of the big hall. Sweet memories, Tom, for it was the billiards room. I clapped my hands in delight and one of the junior officers asked if I ever played billiards to which I said no but have often played another game in a billiard room.

"Two officers came sliding into the room with their arms full of champagne bottles, big ones and not like the little things that they serve you in restaurants nowadays. Iced as well. Whiskey too had been brought in and these were opened also as champagne corks popped for the fizz to spew out over hands and glasses. A full glass was passed across to me and it was lovely and cold to the touch.

"It's bloody hot in here, I cried out and poured the full glass down between my tits. They roared out loud with laughter at this as they slapped each other's backs. Some wag grabbed another bottle and poured it over another fellow's head who then pretended he was under a shower and started rubbing the stuff under his arms. Everybody was laughing and drinking and a fresh glass was put into my hand which tasted good after the dinner wines. I saw one of the younger officers whisper into the captain's ear and he came over to me wavering slightly.

"All's clear, ma-am. Your aunt muttered some threats but she has departed. Bugler! He called. Where's the bloody lad! A young ensign wavered up. Where's your bugle? I didn't bring it into the mess sir. Well pretend you have and sound the call to arms. The ensign was helped up onto a table where he wobbled a bit until he got his balance and put his fist to his mouth and trumpeted out the call to arms.

"The other officers and there must have been about twenty of them in the long billiard room knew just what to do for there was a mad scurrying about as they pushed all the furniture up to the walls including the massive and heavy billiard table. With all the chairs and the like up around the walls it left a big clear space running the whole length of the room.

"The champagne and whisky were placed on the massive mantle above the fire place and it must have been at least three feet wide. I also was helped up onto this ledge along with their glasses of drinks. A couple of hands had a quick feel of me as I was helped up there and a full glass of champagne was passed to me and as I reached down for it, one of my straps came loose and my tit on that side popped out of my dress front. A big roar went up as I struggled up onto my feet and pulled my arm free from the strap so that my arm was bare to my waist and this one tit standing out proud. I bent forward and dipped the nipple into my full glass and then raised up the glass and drank it straight down. The cheers rang out and the captain had to really shout to be heard to call them to order and shouted out to me what the name of the game they were about to play was called. But in the general hubbub, I didn't catch it.

"The officers split up into two teams and a stuffed ball was thrown into the middle of the floor and it appeared that the idea was to get this ball down to the wall at the opposing end of the room. The men stripped of their jackets, those still wearing them, as they lined up at the wall at each end.

"Will you give the word to start, ma-am, the captain called out to me. What do the winners get? I asked. Nothing, ma-am. Nonsense, I cried. There must be a prize, and I raised my voice to a shout. There will be a prize for the winners, and I put my hand up under my exposed tit and pushed it up. The prize for the winners, is, I gave a pause before I shouted out, Me! Now go!

"With a great roar, the two sides hurled themselves forward and what a crashing sound they made when they met in the middle! My God, it was a battle royal! There were no rules that I could see as they just piled into one another. Fist and boots flying as they scrambled for this stuffed ball. A kilt came flying out from this melee. It was a wavering seething mass of bodies and limbs which suddenly shifted about halfway down the length of the room.

"I was jumping up and down at the sight of all those big men fighting for me. My other shoulder strap came loose and the top half of my dress now fell down to my waist, the belt at my waist preventing it from falling down completely. Now both of my tits were out and bouncing about as I jumped up and down in the excitement of the fight and it must have distracted some of them because the whole mass of men suddenly moved again back towards the other end of the room. They came surging past me, trampling over those that had fallen in the first clash leaving two piles of bodies accounting for nearly half of those that had started.

"There was a sudden flurry and the mob moved even closer to the wall and there were shouts of triumph as they got near but they were premature because with a rallying cry they were halted a few feet away from their goal. Those defending and with their backs almost up to the wall heaved and a tumbling mass came roaring down the room carrying along those that had staggered to their feet. Again, with a growing roar, they swept past me stumbling across bodies stretched out and hurled what was left of the opposing team into the far wall with a huge crash.

"I was screaming with delight at seeing this magnificent charge and of the fighting as the stuffed ball was held up against the wall. The gallant captain who was in charge of the winners led what was left of his band to stand down there in front of me. I had refilled my glass and lifted it high, my breasts standing up high with my uplifted arm. A toast, I cried. A toast to the victors and a toast to the valiant losers. I drank it down and tossed the glass out to be caught by one of them as I spread my arms out wide. And for the victors, I cried, the prize, and I launched myself out at them off that wide mantle piece. They caught me before I hit the floor and lucky I was that they did for it was something I would never have done sober.

"Seven men caught me for that was all that was left standing out of forty, well there were a couple of the losing side but they turned their attention to their wounded comrades. They also had the task of dragging the unconscious bodies out into the next room being told to fuck off to let the winners enjoy their prize.

"I was in seventh heaven, Tom, for weeks I'd dreamed of men and that night I had forty of them fighting for me and now I was left with the magnificent seven. When I had landed among them from my leap into their arms, they all had a good feel of my tits and now it was it was getting to the time for the pay off.

"With the floor being cleared of the losers and unconscious winners, I was getting excited as they began to argue as to who was going to be the first to sample my favours, read that as getting to fuck me. The only thing they could agree on was that it should be me to make the choice of the order they would service me in. So I said how about some skill with billiard balls and there were a few groans at this as one said, what rank he was, you couldn't tell now as half of them had lost their shirts and two without kilts. He said that would mean the best player would win and be first.

"Not with the game I've got in mind, I replied. This one you've never played before and anyone of you can win. I'd remembered about the two little plastic balls and thought a variation on this would be a good idea for the contest.

"Fetch out a flat table, I cried, and put one end against the wall. They quickly dragged one over and rammed it against a wall and it was perfect for it was about six foot by four wide. Fine, I said, help me up, and so they got me up onto the table and I stood there with my hands on my hips, my tits up and proud for them to see. Now each got a coloured billiard ball for themselves and two white ones for me. I knew my billiards and that there are seven colours including red but excluding the white so that they would all have a different one. They came back with them. Now, I said, colour by rank. Black to the senior, pink to the next and so on and I'll have the two white ones. They soon sorted out their ranks and colours and stood waiting for my next order.

"Now that you gentlemen have balls, and when the roaring laughter subsided, I carried on speaking. Let's have something to shoot the balls with. One officer started to move over to the cue rack on another wall. Stupid fucker, I shouted out at him. You've got your own fucking cues between your legs. I hope, I added.

"They shouted and laughed and the kilts came off those that were still wearing them for me to see that their cock cues were at the ready. There was laughter among them and shouting at each other. Hey Jock, your cues bent. It'll go round corners! They laughed and made fun of each other until I held up my arms.

Now you can see the pocket to aim at, I said as I undid the belt at my waist and let my dress fall to my feet and kicked it away and opened my legs wide for them see. There were cries of delight as I moved to the back end of the table and sat down with my back to the wall and spread my legs wide apart for them to see my sex. They could see it quite clearly for I knew that the lips were wide open and would be glistening for I was already wet in the anticipation of very shortly being fucked by all seven of them. I dare not touch myself for I knew I would have come there and then and made a mess of the table and the balls would probably have got stuck.

"Well I placed the two white balls in line about a foot away from the target and about six inches apart. Now, I cried, Black first and you mustn't hit the white balls but must sail straight in but can bounce off my legs. No hands remember, it's your pricks that are the cues.

"It was hilarious. The captain put his black ball down on the edge of the table, his prick up hard and jutting out from his thighs. He put the tip of it close to the ball and eased his bum back and then thrust forward and struck the ball. It moved up the table but at an angle and didn't even reach my legs before falling off the edge of the table. The others howled their delight as the pink ball was placed down. This man was so excited that when he thrust his hips forward, he didn't hit the ball at all but stubbed the end of his prick against the table's edge. The jolt to the table made the ball roll sideways and fell as he howled with the pain as the others howled with laughter. I cried out that if a ball stayed on the table, it was to remain where it finished up.

"The blue only just reached the side of my leg and the green did well but touched a white ball and rolled next to the blue. The brown scarcely moved off the line and it sure was a funny sight to see these upholders of the British Empire using their cocks to bat balls down a table at a nice juicy fanny. The yellow rolled halfway down and stopped and it was left to a young subaltern I think with the red ball. There were four balls on the table when his prick hit the red one and sent it up the table at an angle. It hit the yellow and rolled off the edge, but the yellow ball kept rolling and neatly passed the two white balls and gently kissed my lips.

"Groans met this result from the losers while the winner jumped with joy, his cock really bouncing and hoped that the violent movement wouldn't start him coming before I'd had it inside me. He wasn't a tall lad but his cock was big enough for me and I jumped off the table and threw my arms round his neck. Now sort out the order as I get to give the winner his prize of being the first one of you to fuck me. You won't be disappointed for I've got lots of time to make up by missing such fine cocks as yours.

"I had a ball, Tom, or should I say a lot of balls smacking my arse that night as I dragged the young man to a sofa off to one side. I'll only describe the first one as the rest that followed was just fuck, fuck, fuck and more fucking, fucking. We pulled the cushions onto the floor and I fell on them on my back and opened my legs wide to take the first one. My arse was up on two cushions so that my sex was wide open for them all to see and was just waiting and almost begging to be filled with a big erection. God, did I need it. I had a burning itch deep within myself and after the excitement of them men fighting and then the ball game, well I was then more than ready.

"I pulled him down so that he dropped between my legs, his prick standing out fearlessly in front of him. Now, I begged and pulled him down onto me and felt his big cock slide up the juices that were already seeping out of me and felt him slide in and fill me with what I had been waiting so long for. I was so wet he slid in without a tremor and I was transported to heaven and clamped him tight with my legs as he began to move and fuck me. My cunny was like Mother Nature in abhorring a vacuum and welcomed that thick throbbing prick inside my empty cavern and urged him on to fill me with his seed.

"I savaged him, that first one. I bit and clawed him and drove him wild so great was my need. We were oblivious of the other six watching and urging us on as we churned around on the cushions. I felt his cock began to expand and he came inside me as if in flood as he pumped his hips tight up to me, grinding himself against me. It had only taken him a minute or so and I gave out a small cry as he pulled out but he was quickly replaced by the next in line to fill me again as I begged for my release. To spend the energy that had been building up for the last few weeks and it was this second prick that opened the flood gates for me. I came with such force and abandonment that I thrashed about with a delirious joy, oh the ecstasy of the relief and freedom I felt then. My head was whirling as in some fantastic dream. I had pricks as hard as iron everywhere, inside me, touching me, surrounding me. Everywhere I turned my head I could see the men standing or kneeling down around me holding their cocks. Big ones, short ones, fat ones and thin ones, some straight and some crooked. All standing out in homage to me with the balls hanging below them. Balls! I was also seeing balls everywhere and all different colours and of different sizes.

"I think at one stage I pleased five men at once for I seemed to recall lying back on one man who had his cock up my arse. Another was between my legs fucking me up the front and with my head to one side, I had this red haired man's prick in my mouth. With my arms flung back, I had a prick in each hand and we all moved together. I believe I had an orgasm as one came inside my cunny as the other shot his load up my backside. My mouth was filled with the semen of the red haired one and I had the other two send their coming all over my face and arms.

"What a night that was! How many I had and how many times I came, I just cannot remember, but it was a night I'll never forget. I think that there were only three men left standing when we finally came to a finish as it was almost dawn.

"They found my dress for me and fortunately found that I hadn't torn it and they helped me into it, still touching me up, the randy bastards. With the last one pushing my tits back inside I was almost ready to strip off again, but they said that they had to get me back to the palace before it was light. The three of them managed to find uniforms of sorts to wear and they escorted me back.

"I managed to get back to my apartments where the servants ran around like wild things coming back so late with it now being daylight as I must have looked like a really fucked whore. They twitted around and got me undressed and into that bloody great pool they call a bath where they washed and scrubbed me, hair and all. Then out and was dried and bustled over to a couch and made to lie down and they began to massage me all over. Oils, creams and sweet smelling lotions; two of them worked into my skin while another two worked on my hair.

"I found out that they had covered up for me when my aunt had got back by saying that I had retired for the night, not feeling too well and was not to be disturbed until the morning. Now they were trying their best to make me look as though I had spent the whole night sleeping and looking refreshed from the rest.

"Well they succeeded with my outward appearance for my aunt looked in shortly after they had finished and was just being served up with some breakfast. She enquired if I had slept well and if I was feeling better now, saying that I looked better for the early night's sleep. I really felt lousy. The sexual relief and feeling had passed after the servants' pounding and pummelling just leaving me with the aftertaste of wine and champagne taken to excess. My aunt said that she was pleased that I was now feeling better because a special guest was expected to visit the palace and we were to look our best that evening when he was due to arrive.

"The palace was in an uproar all day in making preparations for the visitor. I didn't know who was coming and I didn't bother to ask for I was just thankful that nobody bothered me and I was able to disappear for some time to catch up on my beauty sleep.

"It was late afternoon when the servants woke me up and it was back in that bath again for another bathing session before being dried and powdered ready to be dressed. Not my own clothes, but instead, they brought out garments of a similar kind that they wore, though theirs was of cotton and these for me were of real silk. They were long pieces of a dazzling variety of colours with a lot of delicate stitching along all hems. But they saw to my hair first by being carefully brushed and fixed up at the top so that it was gathered to one side of my head and hung down to cover my left shoulder. This partially covered my face on this side but left the right side clear so that it could be seen, even my ear. I was loaned, they said, a small diamond clip that they attached to the lobe. I was then carefully given a light covering of oil and perfumed before they declared I was ready to be dressed.

"I stood naked and they wound one of the silk pieces round me and simply tucked into itself so that it hung from the waist straight down to the floor. They then held up a delicate silk bodice to put on but I refused to wear it. They twitted about and said that as my top half would only be covered by one thin piece of silken cloth, I should wear the bodice as my tits would show. They didn't call them tits but referred to them as my upper body parts. So what, I retorted! My tits were something to be proud of and I wasn't ashamed of them and it wouldn't embarrass me if people could see them.

"They complained that they would get into trouble if I didn't wear the bodice, but I was adamant and would not put it on. I had them put on this upper silk cloth and insisted that it was put on as it should be if I was wearing that damned bodice. Then I asked to see myself in a full length mirror which was brought into the room for me to see how I looked.

"I could easily have turned into a lesbian if it hadn't been my own reflection I was looking at. Tall and slender with a touch of haughtiness but still gave the impression of hidden sensuous passion that lay behind my smouldering blue green eyes. Head held erect with my features pale and fine upon a smooth delicate white throat and neck to be seen on one side, my dark hair contrasting nicely with its gentle wave coming down the side of my face to curl across the shoulder.

"A pale green silk draped around the shoulders and upper half with one end coming over a shoulder that I held with one crossed arm at the waist leaving my midriff bare. I could see my full firm breasts quite clearly outlined with the dark rings of the aureoles and the nipples standing out clear in profile. Then this gorgeous shade of blue silk moulded to the hips and waist and flowing smoothly down to the floor. I looked and felt like a queen.

"The servants were still protesting about the fact that my tits could be seen when it was time for me to go down to dinner and meet this special guest. I ignored their chatter and left them muttering about how I looked as I left the room to go downstairs

"The place where dinner was being held was a huge circular room with little cushioned alcoves all the way round, each with its own coloured silken drapes. In front of these alcoves were wide steps, four, I think, and these were carpeted and covered in enormous cushions. The large central area, which was left clear, had a marble floor and was very cold to your bare feet. You entered from one end of this circular arena, I always thought of it as such, opposite to where the Rajah, whatever his name was, sat.

As usual, there were many people lounging about on the cushions round the sides when I entered, and there were many small tables in front of them holding fruits, sweetmeats, spices and ornate jugs of water. Everybody was sumptuously dressed tonight, the men in rich brocades and the women with them in their bright silks. I advanced into the arena and the laughing and talk suddenly died away. I held my head up and continued walking towards the steps up to the Rajah's table. I could feel everybody's eyes on my tits as I felt them give their little swaying bounce as I walked forward.

"The Rajah was not seated in his normal place in the exact centre opposite to the entrance but to the left of a man who occupied this place. A very dark and handsome man who wore a bright green turban with a large jewel shining in the centre and an enormous feather sticking up from the back. The Rajah stood up and welcomed me as I went forward to the cushions around the low table, and as I walked up the carpeted steps, I was conscious of the dark man's eyes carefully watching me. The Rajah said how beautiful I looked wearing his country's style of dress, and then introduced me to the other man who had now risen up. He stood about five foot ten but looked even taller with his green turban. He wore a white knee-length jacket, open at the front, that was covered in gold embroidery.

"The silks he wore beneath it were also covered in this delicate work. He was addressed as His Highness by the Rajah, I couldn't repeat all of the title and I only caught the first of it which sounded like Prince Till-I-Come. The hand he held out to me was as dark as his face and on one finger was a large ring with the biggest ruby I've ever seen. I put my hand into his and he bent low and kissed it, the feather in his turban almost tickling the end of my nose.

"'A vision of paradise here on earth,' he said to me in perfect English, giving me a lovely smile showing lovely white teeth. 'Come sit beside me.' He'd been educated in England and his voice was low and melodic. It hypnotised me and kept me entranced the whole evening. I can't remember now a darn thing that he said, only that he spent the entire time talking and looking at me. He didn't even glance at the dancers who went through their whole new elaborate routine that they had devised for this special guest.

"I had caught the disapproving look from my aunt when I first entered but didn't notice her or the Rajah for the rest of the evening.

"When the evening finished, that is, the entertainments were over and most of the hangers-on, that's what I called them, had left, we moved so that the servants could rearrange the cushions, plumping them up to make them soft again, and the tables had been re-laid with fresh fruits and sweetmeats. The Prince went and sat with the Rajah and my aunt and spoke for several minutes. Then my aunt got up and came over and sat down beside me.

"'The Prince has formally asked for your hand in marriage,' she said to me. 'What do I say?' Her eyes were alight with a gleam that I'd never seen before and then realised why she had brought me out with her to this country. It was to find me a rich husband. Well she had found one, but the question was, did I want him?

"I looked up and across the room and saw the intensity, nay, felt the intensity of his gaze. It was direct, alive, and I could see the fires hidden therein. I then noted the lines of passion around his mouth and could see his strong white teeth shining in his dark face and could just imagine the dark strength beneath his fine robes.

"I lifted my head erect and straightened my back, feeling my breasts quiver with the movement below their silk covering and felt my nipples rise to the soft whispering touch of the silk cloth. His eyes shifted fractionally to them and then back up to my face as he waited for my answer.

"'Yes,' I said with a smile and his eyes lit up and he smiled back at me, one that was as wide as Texas. He gracefully and without any apparent effort, rose up from his cushion and sharply clapped his hands twice and then gestured for me to face the centre of the room. Into this arena came a line of retainers bearing armfuls of silks, bottles, jars, casks and chests, carpets and drapes. These last two were spread out just below the steps I was standing on and it was like a tale from the Arabian Nights.

"The caskets and chests were emptied out onto them and I've never seen so many fine jewels and gold that spilled out at my very feet. The fires of light that flashed around us from the coins and the scattered stones were like that of many rainbows being seen at the same time. I nearly creamed my knickers, only I wasn't wearing any. I felt him sit down next to me and he took my hand and pressed it to his lips.

"'This is but a trifle that I would have adorned my wife. This is my dowry to you though it is but a paltry sum for such a beautiful woman that you are. I feel ashamed that I have brought so little for so much that I shall receive.' I felt his eyes on my tits beneath their thin covering. Christ, I thought, seeing all that wealth spread out for me. Bloody good job he didn't see me the night before, being fucked by all those soldiers for he wouldn't have given me a thing then. I could feel that my face was going red as I kept my eyes down.

"'My Lord,' I said. It sounded funny, me saying that, but it came so natural like. 'My Lord. I am too unworthy for such fine things that you have brought me. I said yes for the man himself, not his wealth or possessions.' The way that he had sat down had bunched up the back of his pants so that it was very tight at the front and with my eyes down, I could see quite clearly outlined what he also possessed that was for me. One of the biggest hard-ons I've ever seen on a man. It looked massive, being thick and long and straining against the tight silk at his thigh. He reached out for my other hand to hold and gently brushed my tit as he did so.

"'Till tomorrow night, my sweet,' he said as he kissed this hand.

"Next minute, he was gone. His retainers started repacking all those sparkling gems and the Rajah servants were all twittering about as my aunt came over and helped me up from my cushion and led me out after us bowing to the Rajah. She led me up to my rooms and though she was speaking, I didn't hear a single word, for all I could see in my mind's eye was the size of that cock beneath the silk cloth of his trousers and I was wetting myself with the anticipation of having it inside me. I knew I would be dreaming of that for many months till we would be married.

"It was a bit of a shock when her voice registered, telling me that it would be that very next morning. This alone had penetrated my mind as my aunt carried on speaking.

"'I thought that all was lost when you came into the room looking like the painted harlot Jezebel, but tomorrow you'll be one of the richest women in the world, and a Princess. Think of it!' My aunt exclaimed with a proud look of satisfaction on her face. 'My niece a Princess!' I hadn't thought of that, of being the Princess of Prince Till-I-Come, only of his big cock that was for me. I'll make him come alright and I only hope, no, I was certain that that weapon of his would make me come. I was all wet again at the thought and stayed that way right till the following morning.

"Tom, I'll tell you all about the preparations that went on and off the long drawn out and elaborate wedding ceremony in another letter because I'm so excited now writing about this that I want to tell you what happened.

"They say that a woman's finest hour is when she gets married, well I suppose that's true in most cases, especially to those watching in the congregation, seeing her at her ultimate best in catching her man, but mine was when we got away and into his apartments.

"The servants had withdrawn after preparing the room and the nuptial bed, and me, for His Royal Highness Prince Till-I-Come. I was laid out on this massive silken covered bed with just a thin strip of silk covering my body from his sight. He had been undressed by his valets or whatever they are called except for a pair of wide silken trousers that looked more like pantaloons. He came into the room alone and he'd now dispensed with the turban and I could see that he had very black hair, neatly smoothed back and his big muscular chest was without any trace of hair. His whole body was very dark, not black, but a very deep brown.

"He smiled at me as he approached the bed and I gave out a gasp as he dropped his trousers. His organ was huge! Dark and ponderous and he'd been circumcised, which I believe is part of their religion out here, and the head of it was a deep purple in colour. It swayed heavily in front of him and I could see his ball bag hanging low beneath it. He reached over to me and slowly began to pull down the covering that was over me, first letting my quivering tits with their rigid nipples show, then continued to slowly pull it further down uncovering the rest of my body. His eyes were on my cunt which I could feel was very wet but I kept my hands still and let him look. I was watching his tool sway and waiting anxiously for him to get onto the bed with me.

"'You have a beautiful body, my dear, which I believe has known many men,' he said as he knelt there on the bed next to me. I started to move to him but he held up his hand. 'For me you have the poise, dignity and bearing of a true princess.' His hand started to stroke one of my breasts. 'I myself am not a virgin either and I do not seek virgins for when I bed a woman, it is for pleasure. From now on, this body of yours is mine. Mine and mine alone. Do you understand that?' His stroking hands were driving me mad with lust.

"'Yes, my Lord,' I said, nodding my head.

"'Then my dear, using the English vernacular, let's fuck.'

"He parted my legs and moved across my leg and poised himself between my thighs. He lifted my backside up to rest on his knees and in that position, was able to put the head of his cock inside the lips of my vagina. It was big. His cock I mean. I know that my cunt has been stretched before but not by a cock of that size. He grasped my hips and slid me up his knees, simply pulling me onto his thick shaft. At the angle I was lying, I could feel it trying to tear the walls into my stomach. He was looking at my face as he did this and I flung my arms out wide and my tits began heaving as I gave out a big gasp.

"'My Prince,' I cried out and he laughed and suddenly swung his legs back and fell forward, ramming his whole length into me. My God, I nearly choked. I thought his prick was coming up into my throat. It filled me completely as I'd never been filled before. I felt him draw back to the entrance and ream his way back as he ploughed a deep furrow inside of me. I could hear my juices squish as he mashed his shaft through the lips of my sex. I felt the shifting skin of his prick as he worked it inside.

The pain and pleasure was mixed as we both fell into the rhythm of his stroke. My legs went up high of their own accord and I could feel his heavy ball bag slap against my arse as he buried himself deep within me. My arms went up round his neck, his elbows being alongside my head. How we fucked! And we fucked all night. He was like a stallion and kept coming back for more. I kept pace with him and was more than satisfied for he was the man for me.

TOM LAID the rest of the letter to one side for it was now really late and he was tired. He knew that the busy time was now here and he had to be up early to see to the beginning of the clearing of the land.

His army training helped for he was awake at dawn and after a pee and a wash, got dressed and went down to the diner for an early breakfast. This he'd just finished as a big trailer parked up with a bulldozer on the back and Tom watched as Martin O'Shea, the contractor, got the 'dozer down the ramp of the trailer and parked it up to let the trailer move off.

Tom took him into the camper van and showed him his drawings of how the motel was going to be laid out and then they went back out and with a tin of paint, marked the boundaries that had to be cleared. A dumper truck had arrived and so Martin got to work to begin clearing within this perimeter.

It took three days to clear the site and another three days of drawing out the stumps of the old burnt trees that would be in the way. One day more saw to the levelling off the ground preparatory to the building work.

During this time, Tom had got together with an architect to measure up the site and draw up the plans for the builder to work from. This work was just for the foundations, sewage pipes and plumbing for the base of the motel would be concrete though the cabins themselves would be of timber.

Quite a wide entrance was planned, between two hedges that would be planted before it opened up to where the rooms would be. There would be twelve rooms in three blocks but only ten for occupancy, the other two was for his room and the office.

The first four would be on the left and the second four facing the entrance and the third lot opposite the first four. Now between cabins one and two would be a small locker running through to the back. The same between cabins three and four, five and six, seven and eight and nine and ten. He explained to the builder who had seen the plans, that these were to be for storage of linens etc, but which Tom had other plans for apart from just being storage places.

The first cabin layout was with a door to the left side of the room when viewed from the front, and against that left wall inside would be a dressing table and a small wardrobe beyond it. To the right would be the bed and a window just past the door. The bathroom would be in the far right hand corner so you would go past the bottom of the bed and then turn right to go in. On the left was a shower stall with one side screen, the other end being open without a curtain facing a blank wall. On the right was first, a hand basin and then a toilet pan with a bidet in between, the floor and walls would be tiled. This was the pattern for all the odd numbered cabins while the even numbered ones would be the mirror image of the others, i.e., the door was on the right of the bed on the left etc. In respect of cabin twelve, which was to be the office, a kitchen would be fitted instead of a bathroom while Tom would actually be living in number eleven with a connecting door between the two.

Each of the three blocks would be raised off the ground by about two feet to allow air to circulate and keep them cool in the summer. It would be concrete pilings but clad in wood as all the cabins would be to give the place a rustic air. This under space would be screened with flower beds except for the few steps that led up to each cabin door. Enough room was allowed for there to be a car parked outside each and yet still give enough room for other cars to pass and turn round what would be a small circular centre piece that would have a transplanted tree there to give some shade to any cars that decided to park beneath when it was fully grown.

The builder had objected to the layout of the cabins because of the extra pipe work needed for soil and waste water, but Tom said that he was prepared to pay for this.

So under the supervision of Tom and the architect, the site was pegged out. A digger was brought in to make the holes for the foundations and dig the trenches for the sewage pipes which would link up with the system where the old house used to stand. It took them four months before they had gone as far as Tom had instructed. This being the shells with roofs and boardwalks and all sanitary and electrics fitted and working by himself, he would see to all the furnishings etc.

While all this construction work was going on, Tom had visited the city and posing as a buyer for the construction of a rehabilitation centre, and ordered from a glass manufacturer, ten large one-way mirrors and ten full length mirrors of the same. These he had made, crated and shipped to a warehouse just marked as glass, for delivery by another carrier so that there would not be a connection between him and the motel.

So with the builders finished and off site, it was time for Tom to make his alterations and adaptations to the motel. Being somewhat of an amateur carpenter, was experienced enough to know exactly what he was doing and proceeded to cut holes in every cabin for the mirrors to be installed. They arrived just as he had finished the cutting out and was soon doing the job of installing them. Just taking one cabin as an example. It was a good four foot by three mirror that was fixed into the wall above where the bed would be. In the bathroom and opposite the open ended shower stall, once a blank wall, was now fixed one of the full length mirrors. A person then using the shower could watch themselves as they bathed but would also give a full view to Tom who would be on the other side in the so called linen locker.

He put up curtains on the inside of these lockers so that any light from the cabins would not spill out whenever he opened the outside locker door. These hinges were heavily greased so that no sound would be made when the door was opened.

Also, he changed the light fittings a little so that he could install new infra-red lighting that he added to the existing lights and that they could only be turned on from the inside of the lockers. Cabins one and two he also spent time to make them both sound proof. Other mirrors had been sent which were destined for cabin seven which he dubbed the glass room. Here, heavy duty glass mirrors were used for the floor and other glass for the walls and ceiling. One wall, that opposite the bed, was set with many offset mirrors so that you could see yourself at ten different angles, depending on where you stood.

While doing all this, the furniture and other material he'd ordered began arriving from various sources, so the next cabin to make over was number three. This was to be entirely of leather. The walls and floor he fitted out in tan, the two armchairs already were made with white. The bed was in contrasting black leather, including the headboard and side table coverings and when this was made up with the white cotton sheets, it looked perfect.

Cabin five was like cabin three but all in different hues of fur, though he did get a cheaper variety because it would be rather costly to replace if he used the genuine stuff. Cabin six then boasted a king-sized water bed and even the armchairs were also filled with water.

Cabin four he designed to cater purely for any lesbian visitors or any pair of females that might book in to the motel. This had a large brass bed installed but not of the usual style but being lower than normal. That was because at the foot end, it had two definite phallic designed end posts. The room also had a standard lamp that had two phallic hooks either side about two and a half feet up from the base, this also was of brass. Tom had added two wooden posts a few feet apart and about half a foot away from the bedroom wall. On this wall he'd fitted two large handles, while on the posts, were another two brass phalli of just twelve inches in length and of a greater thickness than the normal male size when fully erect. Just level with these on the wall and directly beneath the handles, were two cup shaped fittings which could support the heels of anybody using it for what it was intended.

As mentioned, cabins one and two were sound proofed because these would cater for people into bondage. In cabin one there were a variety of wall and ceiling hooks and a locked cupboard that held a lot of the paraphernalia associated with this form of sexual practice. Also was cabin two though this had two what looked like pull down beds that closed up to the wall. Well one was a bed but the other was really a cleverly designed rack with all the straps attached.

The remaining three cabins were of the conventional style of room, but they still had the viewing mirrors for Tom's later enjoyment of the standard traveller.

All this took Tom nearly two months to complete his renovations and additions before he was satisfied that the place was now ready to open. This work had taken its toll on Tom for he'd been just too tired to go out at night to see what was happening in the various bedrooms of his neighbours.

He'd already visited the town's local paper and placed an advert in giving the date of the opening and also a few of the papers up in the city. He had not wanted anything official like a pompous ceremony and all that went with it, but just a quiet opening day. So after an early breakfast in the diner, he strolled back and looked with pride on what he had built. He turned as the daily convoy begins to pass carrying those men to their jobs in the city. There was some tooting of horns as they passed and he waved back at them in acknowledgement. Almost every evening on the way back, they would have sport with the local state highway police who were on traffic patrol.

It had started many years ago and took time to develop. Those men that travelled up to the city had got together and started buying exactly the same cars. They got into groups of four for sharing, taking their turn to drive every four weeks, but they all had bought a similar car in respect of style and colour. So the town itself had over sixty black sedans parked on the driveways or garaged all over town. It was on the drive home that they had their fun as they formed up in a convoy, but one car would lag behind. Then he would come roaring down the highway doing well over the speed limit, past the stationary state trooper which would immediately give chase. They had it down to a fine art, for as the speeding black sedan came into sight, a gap would appear in the convoy and it would slip in and continue on in the sedate speed of the others. The police on numerous occasions would pull them all over but could never positively identify which of those cars was the culprit. Even when a car was chased into town, with so many black sedans parked on the drives, they could never pick out the one they had been chasing. It made for a good laugh in the club at the weekend that they'd fooled the police yet again.

Only one car had ever been identified, and this was when Tom was overseas, and that was because at the peak of the chase, it had a front tyre burst. This sent the car off the highway doing over a hundred miles an hour, cart wheeling and crushing the occupants until it finished up jammed in a small ravine. The police car hadn't seen it go off the road and it was two days before other people from the town found the vehicle with the dead men inside. One of those dead had been Yeovil Yates and his death had sent his wife a little loopy. But that accident hadn't stopped the others from continuing this sport over the years.

Tom waved as they went off and hoped that some other cars on the return run, not necessarily theirs, might stop for the night at his motel. He went on into the office and for the first time, switched on the outside illuminated sign showing that the Love Motel now had vacancies.

IT WAS late afternoon before the first car pulled in for an early night stop. The driver was allocated cabin number nine, one of the normal ones, and then had a second car stop with what looked like a man and his wife. They got cabin ten, and this was before it was even dark. He'd told them that there was a diner just a few yards down the road if they wanted to eat.

Then the convoy passed, tooting again as they did so, knowing that this was his first day of being open, and it was shortly after this that a local man pulled in. Tom was surprised to see that it was Fred Willis, a manual worker from the small local foundry. Keeping the surprise from his face, Tom went into the office with Fred following and went behind the counter before turning round to face him. Fred had appeared to sidle into the office and then shuffled over to the counter to stop in front of Tom.

'Er…hello, Tom. I…er, heard in town that you've just opened this here motel,' he said with a slight stammer, not looking Tom in the eye. 'I wondered…I wondered if I could have a room for the night…if you know what I mean. I…I've got a bit of a problem, and I…er, want, er, a night away from home.'

'No problem, Fred,' Tom replied, opening the register. 'Put down what you like, though the only cabins available are a bit above the normal price for a motel room because they are somewhat on the special side,' giving him a grin, 'if you know what I mean. How about cabin six? It's got a nice large water bed. Chairs too?'

'That sounds great,' Fred, interrupting Tom from saying any more. 'I'll take it,' he said, taking out his wallet and paying the amount asked without question. 'Thanks, Tom,' he said, picking up the key, 'you're a real pal.' Tom grinned as he put the money away in a drawer, never having really been a pal of Fred when growing up in the town.

'It's in the top section, second cabin from the right. Do you want to book an early morning call?'

'No, thanks, we'll…er,…I'll be alright. You know me,' he replied with a sheepish grin as he left the office.

Tom watched him return to his car and drive off to the far end, but couldn't see who the other person was inside the vehicle. No matter, he thought, I'll soon find out in a minute or two he smiled, but another car pulled up at that moment and a weary traveller came and booked in. So it was nearly ten minutes before Tom could leave the office and make his way round to the locker between cabins five and six. Though the three blocks of cabins made up three sides of a square, they were still connected by a covered boardwalk all the way round, very similar to the way the western towns of old were built.

He silently moved round towards that locker between five and six, his stealth was not deliberate, for it was now natural to him from years of practice from his early boyhood days of moving through the back gardens at night. The door opened easily and quietly as the grease and oil had intended that it be so. He locked the door behind him and went and drew the curtain from the two way mirror above the bed. Light flooded the locker and it made Tom shrink back to the shadows at the side, fearing that all his work had been in vain and that he could be seen.

Peering round the corner of the mirror, he saw Fred come out of the bathroom, bollock naked as he strode to the bed. Tom looked down and saw this gorgeous red headed woman lying spread eagled on the bed. Natural colour, he noted, seeing the same red hair between her thighs; big breasts with almost an identical shade to the aureoles surrounding the nipples. She was unknown to Tom, but he knew for certain that it definitely wasn't Fred's wife.

She gave out a luscious delightful giggle as Fred knelt on the bed, making the water move and send her body into undulating movements, her tits especially, wobbling about like two jellies on a plate.

'Some bed, eh?' Fred grinned at her.

'It's wonderful,' she giggled again. 'How clever of you to find this place. I think we'll enjoy ourselves on this,' she said, raising her arms for Fred to move in on top of her, his erection disappearing between her legs as he mounted her, stopping her giggles by kissing her.

Tom watched as they fucked, and getting bolder, he stood in the middle of the mirror and watched as they bucked and bounced on the water bed till they both came with shrieks and groans. It was with a wet sucking sound that their bodies came apart as Fred got off the girl, his face flushed with the exertions. The girl got off the bed, giving a giggle as she literally bounced off it to make her way to the bathroom.

Tom moved along the locker and opened the curtain to look inside the bathroom. The girl had squatted on the bidet and was washing her lower parts as the curtain opened. He watched as she dried herself and flinched as she approached the full length mirror which he was behind. She stood very close and moved her naked body different ways, admiring herself, pushing her large breasts together and then stroking the erect nipples. Tom moved and stood just before her, marvelling that he could stand so close, within touching distance and yet not be seen. His erection was hard in his hand as he masturbated right in front of her as she kept posing before him as she touched various intimate parts of her body. He splattered the mirror, but didn't dare clean if off in case the mirror itself moved, but would clean it the next day.

He pulled the curtain closed as she left the bathroom and he was just in time to see her bounce onto the bed, nearly sending Fred to the floor from the undulating wave of water beneath him. He chuckled to himself at her squeals of pleasure as they bounced together on this bed and Fred rolled her over onto her back.

'Ready for more?' he asked, his cock standing upright again.

'When have I never been ready, honey?' she asked, spreading her legs for Fred to mount her again. The bed moved beneath his thrusting in and out, but he kept losing momentum as the water had its own motion until he adapted to pushing down hard into her and waiting for her to bounce back, taking all of him inside her.

'Some fucking bed, eh baby,' he said, watching her tits move as though they had batteries inserted to make them vibrate.

'You said it, honey! Some fucking bed. Harder, harder, fuck me harder,' she pleaded.

'I'm doing my best,' he grunted.

'Then let me get on top,' she cried, rolling him over so that she could get astride him. Then she cried with delight as he bounced up tight into her, the water bed helping them. Tom smiled as he pulled the curtain closed, pleased with the comments they had made about the bed.

Though he didn't know it at the time, Tom had just seen Fred on his best behaviour. It was a couple of months later that he saw the worst side of him. He liked cabin six and became a frequent visitor for that particular cabin. Again it was another female that Tom had never seen before and they were lying in the sixty nine position on the bed. Fred was on his back licking her out while she sucked on his erection, when he suddenly grasped her hips and pushed her up as he came up into a sitting position. Here he proved how strong he was by lifting her up by the hips, her mouth still clamped firmly round his prick, raised her up in an upside down position. He did this so quick, the poor girl had no chance with his cock still stuck in her mouth as he held her upside down whilst still on him as she started to gag.

'Keep your head well back,' he growled at her, 'and you won't choke. Just relax your throat.' She had to do just that to be able to breathe. Holding her tight, her legs in the air, he lifted her up and down, using her as a pump on his prick, and by keeping her head back, was able to take the whole length of him deep down into her throat, her nose touching his balls. Tom could see the outline of Fred's prick through the skin of her throat jumping about as he shot his load deep inside.

He then, when finished coming, lifted her off and dropped her onto the bed. The water contained inside acted as a spring and it bounced her clear off and out onto the floor. She sat up, her breasts heaving as she massaged her throat, red in the face from the suffused blood, gasping for air. She crawled to the side of the bed and leaned against the side.

'You bastard,' she whispered. 'You lousy fucking bastard,' her voice croaking. Without any apparent movement, he gave her a back handed swipe that knocked her back onto the floor, where she now lay but rubbing her face and head now.

'That was great, honey, just great, only don't ever call me a bastard. You said that you liked a man that could do things to a woman.

Well I just did something that I bet no man has ever done to you before. And what's more, you'd have enjoyed it even better if you had relaxed instead of the soft way of playing about that you were doing earlier.'

Tom got to know that this was true over a period of time, seeing Fred do this to quite a few females. The first time he did this to a girl was always the worst, and yet he'd finish up with the girl's begging for him to do it time and time again.

Delving further into the future in regards to cabin six involving the water bed, led to a slight change, though it was a major one at the time. One of the town's local whores, who worked during the day in the laundry, would occasionally come to the motel with her pick up in tow. The punter had to pay the rent for the session. She was, well let us not say she was really overweight, but she was extremely fat. This weedy looking man had come into the office specifically to book cabin six for the night. Tom could see who he had outside in his car and had no hesitation in charging the special price for that cabin and felt sorry for this small little man. He took the money and handed over the key and soon followed them to slip into the locker to watch how this little runt of a man would cope with the mammoth woman he'd got for the night.

He couldn't have been much over five foot in height and when stripped down, looked like a reject from Belsen. It was the tool that hung down between his legs that astounded Tom. The man was hung like a donkey, and it was unbelievable that a human could have a dong that size. His daily intake of food must have been just to supply that length of flesh that almost hung to his knees. It was thicker than his scrawny forearm.

She was the exact opposite of him. One thigh alone was thicker than his torso and just one breast was bigger than his head. She had undressed and somehow flopped and rolled herself into the middle of the water bed, which for her size, was no mean feat. The bottom sheet had moved and you could see the water through the clear plastic trying to find a new level with her weight displacement, the sides bulging our rather alarmingly as she beckoned to the scrawny thing standing out in the middle of the room.

He had an erection, but so huge was his cock that he didn't have the stomach muscles to be able to hold the thing out in front of him. It still hung down between his legs, stiff and rigid, the huge head almost level with his knees and nearly the same size as his kneecap. He hefted the enormous thing with one hand which would have made any jenny tremble and blush. He managed to get onto the water bed and stood up, trying to steady himself till the water settled down before he placed himself between her small feet.

Yet her small feet and trim ankles surprised Tom, considering the size and weight of her body they had to support, and they were now spread as far apart as she could manage. In spite of the distance between her two spread feet, her body flesh came together about half way up her thighs. The poor man couldn't have seen what he was aiming for as there was a foot thick of flesh to plough through before getting to his goal, but plough he did. He plucked up courage from somewhere, and holding that fleshy stake of a cock, gave a strangled cry and fell forward. The shaft of his tool disappearing between the folds of flesh and must have found his buried target because she gave a heave on the bed and his head disappeared between her massive tits.

He must have found it because she started bucking up and down while she pressed her hands into his lower back so that she didn't bounce him off. He fought and struggled and finally managed to get his hands down and lift his head free, his face bright red as he gasped in a lungful of air before disappearing again into her tits.

Both his knees were planted on her thighs as he could never had straddled her as his arse went up and down like a fiddler's elbow. She was doing her bit too by bouncing up and down as fast as he was.

Whether he shot his load or she had an orgasm, Tom didn't know, because the bed just couldn't take it. With a muted crack, it disintegrated in an explosion of water with the pressures that were being exerted on it. Tom rubbed frantically on the window, trying to remove the water that was obscuring his vision, which of course he couldn't, it all being on the other side. It was a good half minute before the water drained down off the glass for him to see clearly into the room. This was now awash and the woman lay there like a drowned fat white slug, and un-believingly, the little fellow was still pounding away. He must have been unaware of what had happened and it wasn't until he raised his head for more air he saw the sopping face and wet bedraggled hair did he realise that something had happened.

The poor little sod hadn't even felt the bed give way.

Tom laughed so much at the sight of the fellow's face that he lost his erection as the fat woman pushed the man off. It took her several rolls on the wet floor before she could get up onto her knees. With her soaking wet hair straggled about her face, her massive arse swaying about and her huge tits brushing the floor, she was a sight to behold. But she still wasn't to be denied as she beckoned the little man over to her. He tentatively approached her, his organ still huge and hot in his hand. With a mouth as big as her arse, opened it and took his cock head in and finished him off.

Tom was ready by the door as they made to leave, standing in a pool of water and expressing dismay at the ruined water bed and damage to the room. The little man stammered out that his watch strap had somehow got caught and ruined the bed. He pulled out his wallet and pushed enough money into Tom's hand that meant that not only could he get the room cleaned, but a better reinforced bed for the cabin. But that was a future event for that particular cabin.

So in his first day of opening, Tom had four cabins occupied. It didn't take long before he got the boss of some local concern booking in for a quickie with his secretary before going home. The cabins let for this purpose was one of the conventional ones, and sometimes could be let up to three times before it became occupied for the night.

He didn't have to advertise for as time went on, it was soon known in the city and he began to get people booking over the phone in the morning to reserve a specific cabin for the night. So within a couple of weeks, he quite often had to switch on the no vacancy sign quite early in the evening.

One night, by six o'clock, two of the ordinary cabins had been booked as well as two of the specials, when George Wrexham phoned. He was a big brawny man and a teacher at the local school. He'd arrived just before Tom finished there, so he knew him. It was a school during the day, but passed itself off as a college in the evenings, generally between five and eight for those wishing to further their education. He taught biology and seemed to take it a step further on the physical side on a one to one basis. He became a regular customer and preferred the glass cabin where he would bring a young female student for further study on the subject. He booked the room, but Tom seldom watched him because the young chicks that he took in there didn't have much experience, but it was sometimes nice to watch his technique.

It was cabin four that was just booking in that interested Tom and would be well worth watching. The one who signed the register as Mary and Jane Thomas, was tall, blonde and had a beautiful round face framed by these wheat coloured locks. She had a very nice figure covered with clothes that looked quite classy. She had asked for a cabin for her and her sister for the night. Tom could see the sister, the names not fooling him, sitting outside in the car, judging her to be as tall but with jet black raven hair, looking just as good as the girl before him.

'Are you very close as sisters?' Tom asked. 'What I mean is, would you like a large bed or two singles. If you are close, or would like to be very close, I have the perfect room that has some tasteful decorations that might appeal to you both.' Her lips parted in a sweet knowing smile showing perfectly formed white teeth.

'Yes, we are very close and a large bed is what we would like, and I'm sure the room you have in mind will be perfect for us.'

She finished signing the book and paid for the room and Tom then escorted her to cabin four and showed her in.

'Perfect,' she said, turning to Tom, her eyes having taken in the bed with its phallic end posts. 'Perfect! We won't stop now, but go into town for dinner and then come back for the night. Thank you,' she said, taking the key from him and going back to her car. Tom returned to the office and watched as the car drove off for them to have dinner and thought that they would be worth waiting for.

Later, with all the cabins let and the no vacancy sign lit, Tom locked the office and made his way to the locker between cabins three and four. He was just entering the locker when he saw their car pull into the motel's entrance. He locked the door behind him and pulled open the curtain just before the girls entered the cabin.

The blonde came in first carrying a small overnight case, putting on the lights, which being carefully hidden in the walls, gave off a very subdued glow, making the polished brass of the bed give off a very warm golden sheen. The other black haired girl followed her in and was just as good looking as the other and could just possibly be passed off as being a sister.

'This is lovely and just look at that bed! Oh honey, where did they find it?' She crossed the room and her shapely hand caressed the upright brass organ at the foot of the bed. Both hands then went on it and moved up and down on the post. 'It's beautiful,' she purred, and dropping to her knees, put her mouth down on the head of the phallic post. 'Mmmmm,' she mouthed.

'Later, darling,' said the blonde, opening the case and taking out a toilet bag and nightie and placed them on the dressing table. She then peeled off her dress to reveal her black bra and panties which were of sheer nylon. The centres of the bra were missing and the nipples of her splendid tits were standing out quite plainly.

'I'll use the bathroom first,' she said, picking the things up from the table, disappeared from the room. Tom heard the shower tap turned on, but stayed to watch the dark haired girl start to strip. With her shoes kicked off and her outer clothes shed to reveal her underwear, which by contrast, were all white. She looked around for somewhere to hang her dress and spied the hooks on the posts but surmised correctly that they weren't for clothes. She looked at these male organ replica hooks and her tongue came out and slowly crept round her full red lips.

She turned her head to glance in the direction of the bathroom where the blonde girl could be heard singing softly above the noise of the water from the shower. The girl in the room made her decision and dropping her dress on the floor, quickly slid her panties down from her hips and stepped out of them. She went to the nearest post hook and knelt down before it, and holding it with both hands, took as much a possible of it into her mouth. Her head went up and down on it as her hips squirmed as she made it as wet as possible with her saliva before releasing it and standing up. She grasped one of the handles on the wall and gave it a tentative tug.

Tom grinned and said to himself that she'd never be able to pull that off the wall. He'd fixed it properly and it would take nearly a quarter of a ton to pull it free.

She stood close to the hook and taking a firm grasp of one handle, arched her body forward and lifted the leg on that side up and placed her heel in the fitted cup. She then grasped the other handle and swung herself up, putting her other heel in the other cup and slowly lowered herself down onto the phallic hook. She threw her head back as her body came into contact with it and sighed as she slowly slid down onto it, taking the whole twelve inches up inside her.

Then by flexing her knees, she moved up and down, the polished brass cock going in and out of her vagina. The cords of neck stood out and a groan escaped from her lips as she moved faster and orgasmed. She stopped and held this position for a few moments before letting one leg fall down from the wall and planting it firmly on the floor. Tom saw that he had been just about right in the positioning of the brass cock as her other foot came down and she let go of the handles and arched her back, pressing her stomach against the post, impaled now on that golden penis. Another groan came out as she moved her body slowly from side to side, really working the hook inside her. Her arms were outstretched and she looked just like a butterfly pinned to a collectors' board.

Tom had got into a right fuzz watching her perform on the brass cock that he jerked himself off so hard that he banged his own cock against the wall and shot his load down the leg of his trousers. When he looked up into the room again after cleaning himself, saw that the girl had taken herself off the totem and had just finished wiping it and was now starting to clean herself with a towel which she threw into the closet when that was done.

At this point, the blonde girl appeared from the bathroom wearing a short see-through nightie. The fringe of this garment fell to her crotch so it couldn't be seen properly, but her full breasts were clearly visible with the dark nipples pushing their way forward.

'The bathroom's all yours now, Mary,' she said.

'Thanks,' she replied, crossing the room, unclipping her bra as she went, throwing it onto the bed but pausing to take out of the case her toilet bag and lightly tripping off into the bathroom.

The blonde, Jane was the name Tom recollected from the signing of the register, sat down at the dressing table and started to file her nails. She also lit up a cigarette and let it droop from her lips, the smoke curling lazily up around her head in the now warm air of the cabin. She was abstractedly running the file across her nails when she noticed the brass cock hooks.

She stopped in mid file as she really looked at them before putting the file down and her cigarette in the ashtray before getting up and moving over to them. She ran her hands over the two phalli and as Mary had done, glanced towards the bathroom but had a different plan of approach. She turned round, facing in towards the room and Tom as she hitched up her nightie. She had shaved herself so what Tom saw couldn't really be called a pussy and couldn't think what it should be called as she parted the hairless crack with her fingers and backed up to one of the cocks and impaled herself on it. Tom had watched as she had lifted one leg and watched the bulbous head disappear inside her and then the rest slowly go in as she slid down on it.

With the golden horn fully inside her, she dropped her head down, the blonde hair swinging past her shoulders as she started to wiggle her bottom from side to side and then backwards and forwards as she was firmly stuck on the pole. She bucked and jerked about, her head swinging from side to side as she worked herself up into a frenzy of motion until she suddenly went rigid and motionless for a few moments. She shuddered and then, slowly and it seemed, reluctantly moved up and forward and nearly fell to her knees as she came free from the pleasurable tool that had serviced her. She cast a look around and picked up a small hand towel and wiped herself and the hook before looking where to dispose of it. She opened the closet door to throw it in there and saw one towel already inside on the floor of it just as Mary came out of the bathroom.

'You used that, didn't you?' said Jane as she pointed to one of the hooks and indicated the towel on the closet floor.

'So did you,' she laughed as she pointed at the towel that Jane was still holding in her hand. Jane laughed with her and threw her towel into the closet and closed the door and held out her hand. Mary, wearing a similar nightie to Jane's, walked over and took the proffered hand. Dressed, if it could be called that, in almost the same attire, did look like sisters in spite of the different hair colouring.

'Darling,' Jane breathed, drawing Mary to her, each holding the other's hand now as they came close together. As their bodies touched, they gently brought their lips to each other and kissed with a smouldering passion.

Tom was carried away with the sheer beauty of the picture the two of them made standing there, their heads slightly to one side as they slowly kissed. The gentle lines of their stretched throats that ran into the nightie where the nipples of their breasts lightly touched each other. The straight lines of their nighties that just revealed the lower curves of the cheeks of their bums. The firm thighs of their smooth legs that swelled out slightly at the calves before tapering to slender ankles and the toes that also were touching each other.

The spell broke as the kiss came to an end, and hand in hand, they moved over to the bed. Mary slowly lifted up the hem of Jane's nightie and pulled it free from her arms and lifted it off over her head, the blonde locks falling back into place as Mary dropped it onto the floor. Jane then did the same for Mary, who, when free from her nightie, laid her fulsome body across the bed with her arms out flung. Her breasts still stayed rounded in this supine position, the nipples standing out proud from their aureoles. Jane placed her hands either side of the prone body before her and lowered her mouth onto one of the heavy breasts.

'Love me dearest, love me,' Mary murmured as she closed her eyes to enjoy what Jane was about to do. Jane's head left the breast and her tongue weaved a crazy pattern down across the taut skin of the stomach. Her tongue went in and around the navel and down to the fringe of pubic hairs. Mary's legs opened for Jane to move in between them, and using her teeth, nibbled her way through the soft brush to the throbbing and now moist crevice. Her tongue and teeth found the small bud in there and alternately licked and nibbled upon it. The edge of Mary's hand went into her mouth as she twisted her head from side to side as she moaned at the sensations she was getting. Jane, her blonde hair swirling about, really worked her tongue into Mary and at the same time, caressed the body with her hands, scalding the skin with the tips of her fingernails. The body on the bed shuddered as she spent herself in a flooding orgasm, her legs coming together and involuntary trapping the head down there doing the service.

Then Mary suddenly sat up and pulled Jane up and on top of her as she fell back, Jane's mouth glistening from the juices and they kissed fiercely so that Mary's own mouth became covered in her own body fluid too. She then rolled Jane over and started to do the same for her.

It had been a long time since Tom had seen two lesbians having a session and knew that this one had been a good one. That they loved each other was obvious and they seemed to be giving each other a great deal of mutual pleasure. He sighed and wished that at some time he could have been a girl just to get the experience and know of the sensual delight that they were both getting, but it wasn't possible for all he could do was watch and play with himself as he did so. He drew the curtain and quietly slipped out of the locker room and locked the door behind him. It was still too early for him to turn in as he wasn't really tired, and having masturbated, thought he would give old widow Yates a look in, but we are not going to say what he saw. He preferred to watch straight sex. Man and woman, woman to woman or man to man, so he wouldn't visit her for a long time now. He made his way into the motel's grounds and decided to have one more look in at the two girls in cabin four. He quietly let himself into the locker room and opened the curtain above the bed.

The sight that greeted him, pleased him so much that he got and instant hard on and as he fumbled to get himself out of his trousers, came and shot his load before he'd managed to free it as both girls were impaled on the two brass cocks at the foot of the bed. He could see the golden shaft going up inside Jane quite clearly, her shaven mound giving a good view. The inner and outer lips were getting red from the work out she was giving it.

The shaft that Mary was using was glistening with the smearing of her juices as she moved up and down on her side of the bed. They were holding hands as they moved up and down in the same rhythm, the golden cocks disappearing and reappearing as they fucked themselves. Their full breasts were moving as much if not more than their hips as they both began to move faster, taking the post right up inside themselves.

'I'm coming, I'm coming, oh God I'm bursting,' Mary screamed out, breaking contact of Jane's hand. She was now standing flat footed across the corner of the bed, stuck on her phallus, her head thrown back and her hands pressing alongside her ears. Her breasts were now quivering with the excitement as the fluid from her body ran down the post. She sagged a little and gave out a short scream and straightened up again, her head falling forward and her hands hanging limp at her sides. Jane then went through the same motions, head flung back and went into a rigid stance as she pumped out her juices down both the shaft and her own leg.

She managed to get off the slippery horn and with difficulty, helped Mary get off her golden joy. They held each other upright in an embrace for a few minutes before moving and collapsing onto the bed.

'What a fuck,' Mary moaned. 'I came and came and came. I didn't think I was going to stop. My God I'm shattered.' Jane put out her arm and pulled the dark head close into her and they nestled together. 'Hold me. Hold me tight and never let me go,' one of them said. 'I love you, love you,' the other murmured. They lay holding each other, utterly spent, breasts squashed between them as they gently stroked each other. Tom closed the curtain and cleaned himself up as best he could with his handkerchief before letting himself out and relocked the door as he carefully did each time. He wandered out into the middle and stood by the growing tree as he looked around with a sense of pride, his gaze taking in the cabins, with lockers, his own room and the office. Mine, all mine, he said to himself. Planned and built by me, well not exactly true, as the construction gang did the hard graft while he put the finishing touches to it. Better than that bloody hotel in the city that his aunt used to have years ago, he mused as he went off to his own cabin.

WITH HIS normal daily routine, Tom was up early to see the guests off the premises and collect the keys. The two "sisters" stopped and thanked him, saying it was the most comfortable motel they had ever stayed in and it would be a definite stopping point for them in the future. They said that they would also recommend it to their friends if they should ever come down this way. He thanked them for their custom, and under his breath, thanked them for the pleasure he had derived from watching them.

With the last of them gone, Tom went and had breakfast down at the diner and was back at the motel an hour later. Now was his time to get fresh linen out of the lockers and place it inside each cabin for his daily help that always arrived about ten to clean the cabins and remake the beds with the fresh sheets etc, that Tom had put out. All the dirty towels and the rest, she put into a hamper in the office for collection later by the regular laundry service from the town.

With the fresh linen out and the daily help having started, he returned to the office and turned on the small television set he had there and tuned in to the local news. The main item was a report of a bank hold up in the city and that the robbers, a male and female, both in their late twenties, had made a successful getaway in an old dark blue Chevrolet. Both were armed and considered dangerous, the news reader said and the programme went onto the adverts.

Tom tuned them out and concentrated on his book keeping.

He was surprised to see, ten minutes later a car pull up outside the office for he didn't usually get vehicles stopping till the afternoon, and late at that. A young man got out of the car and stretched himself before entering the office. Tom noted that he looked a little bleary eyed which the fellow pointed out that he and the wife were stopping early for he'd been up all night.

Tom got him to sign the register and took the cash and gave him the key to cabin number seven, the mirrored cabin. He watched him walk back out to the car and move it off to park and then noted that it was a dark blue Chevrolet, and with a woman in it too. This brought the TV news to mind and so he waited until they had gone inside the cabin before he quickly made his way down there and went into the locker between that and number eight.

'This sure is some room, Wayne,' he heard the woman say before he'd even gotten the door locked behind him. 'If I wasn't wearing panties I'd be able to see my snatch.' Tom drew back the curtain from the mirror above the bed and saw her standing in the middle of the room with her legs wide apart looking down at her reflection from the mirrored floor. 'I'll even be able to watch you hump me,' she said, looking up at the ceiling.

'I'll be able to watch myself too,' he said with a laugh as he looked at the wall of the bathroom, beginning to take his clothes off.

'How much do you think we got?' she asked, lifting one of two holdalls onto the bed.

'I don't know,' he said as his trousers came off to reveal that he had an erection. The young woman then opened the bag and emptied it out onto the bed and hundreds of dollar bills cascaded onto the cover.

'Wheee,' she exclaimed excitedly. 'There must be over twenty grand here,' as she spread it out to look at it.

'It makes for a pretty fucking bed. So get that dress off and let's celebrate,' he said, picking up the second holdall and putting it inside the closet as she quickly pulled off her dress and panties and threw herself onto all the money and rolled over onto her back and looked up at the glass ceiling.

'What do you love most, me or the money?' she asked as the man stood there looking at his profile in the wall mirror, his cock jutting out from his thighs.

'Both,' he said, getting onto the bed and between her open legs and quickly stuffing his prick inside to begin fucking her.

Tom now knew that these two must be the bank robbers and wondered what to do as he watched them humping away on top of all that money on the bed. He also got to see her tits for the man on top had put both hands up and pushed her bra up to her neck so that he could feel her breasts against his chest. This delayed Tom for he pulled out his own erection now and began to use his hand as he watched the two fuck and the man try to suck on a teat as he moved inside her. Tom could imagine the thrill they were getting and he leaned his head against the glass as he reached his peak and came all over the wall before they even finished themselves. He cleaned the head of his cock with a handkerchief as he heard her cries of an orgasm and the grunting sounds of the man as he came at the same time. One more glance through the mirror saw they were stationary now and breathing heavily as he pulled the curtain closed and quickly left the locker to go back to the office. He picked up the phone and dialled a number.

'Sheriff Rivers?' he asked when the phone was picked up at the other end. 'Yes, it's Tom Love at the motel out on the highway. I think I've got those two bank robbers from the city in one of my rooms. A young man and a woman and they have a dark blue Chevrolet. They also had a holdall that I think is full of money. Yes. Yes,' he answered to questions asked. 'But no sirens please. I don't want a shoot out here. Okay, I'll meet you at the front with a key.' He put the phone down and saw that his hand was trembling. He went to a small cupboard and took out a duplicate key to cabin seven and went and waited outside the motel's entrance.

Five minutes later, the town's two police cars came out of Lincoln Avenue and pulled up near Tom and out of sight of the interior of the motel. Four officers got out, one being the sheriff who walked over to Tom.

'Hi Tom, so you reckon they are the robbers then?' he asked.

'I do,' Tom said. 'They're in cabin number seven, second from the right at the end. Here's the spare key.' He handed it over and they must have talked this over before arriving for they split up into pairs without saying a word and approached round the back of the cabins on both sides, guns drawn and inched their way towards cabin number seven.

The two who'd approached from the window side of the cabin, crouched down below the sill as the sheriff slowly inserted the key into the lock and just as carefully turned the key. Then he quickly pushed the door open and dived in with his gun held out in front of him followed by the other three.

'Freeze!' he yelled out, and Tom could just see over the shoulder of the last deputy, the young couple still naked on the bed and still lying on all the money from the holdall.

The woman gave out a scream as her partner rolled off of her, pulling himself out of her quite violently. His prick still up hard and now all shiny with her juices.

'Don't even think about it,' the sheriff snarled as he saw the man's head turn towards the bedside table that had a gun on the top. He slowly moved round the bed as he still had his gun stretched out in his hand covering them though they also had three other guns pointing in their direction. The sheriff picked up the gun and stuck it in his belt.

'Now get off the bed, slowly, the pair of you,' he said as he stepped back to give the man room. This man had a look of bewilderment on his face as he slowly swung his legs off the bed and the girl had a look of pure hate in her eyes as she too, slowly began to move rolling onto her side to get up.

Tom was in a good position at the door to see her hand slide under the pillow as she pushed herself up and came up with a gun in her hand. She fired it at the nearest police officer and he was thrown back to bounce off the door post as the other officer covering her fired his gun and the bullet caught her in the throat. But even as she was thrown backwards herself, she managed to pull the trigger again and hit the one that had shot her.

This triggered off the sheriff and the other deputy to fire their guns but at the man instead. One bullet took him in the head while the other went into the middle of his chest. The head shot took his brains out and splattered them over the mirror on the bathroom wall as well as shattering that as pieces of glass flew everywhere. Most of it falling down onto his body than had been flung against it.

The noise had been deafening in the confined room and Tom was aghast at the blood and glass that the room was now covered in. The air was full of cordite smoke and the sweet heavy smell of blood and gore and even though he'd seen combat in Korea, it still made him feel sick to see it happening yet again. What was even worse was that it was in his very own place that he'd witnessed it.

He saw at once that the deputy that had been shot first was dead and so he went to the aid of the other one who was swearing to blue blazes as he gripped his right shoulder as blood oozed out between his fingers. At a glance he saw the girl on the bed was dead, her eyes glazed as blood still pumped out of her throat to run down between her naked breasts. He couldn't see the other man from where he was kneeling but saw the sheriff use his boot to kick him, swearing himself before he turned round to help Tom.

'Get on the radio,' he shouted to the one standing deputy. Shouting, because like all of them, his hearing had been somewhat impaired by the blasting of the guns. 'Get two ambulances here double quick.' As the deputy rushed out to go to their cars, the sheriff came over and knelt down next to Tom.

'How is he?' he asked.

'Shoulder wound. He'll live,' Tom said getting to his feet.

'Fucking bitch!' the wounded man said between clenched teeth as he grimaced. Tom looked at the mess of the room, seeing the girl spread eagled on the bed, her legs wide open as if inviting sex. Tom was glad to notice that the bullet that killed her hadn't gone through the wall into the locker and could now see the slumped body of the man amidst the glass of the shattered mirror. The other deputy came back into the room pushing the woman cleaner out of the way who'd come over to look.

'Here in ten minutes,' he panted to the sheriff.

'Give me a hand to get Joe outside ready,' the sheriff said to him.

'No!' said Tom. 'It's better not to move him till the medics get here. You might make things worse by moving him.'

'Okay,' said the sheriff. 'now where's that holdall you mentioned?' he asked of Tom. They both looked towards the dressing table and there by the side was the empty bag. Tom swung round and only then noticed that the money was still on the bed.

'There's the money,' he said to the sheriff.

'Oh shit,' he exclaimed. 'Pass me the bag.' He began collecting what he could and stuffing it inside and then got the other deputy to roll the girl over so that he could collect what she had been lying on. Quite a few of the notes had blood on them but he gathered it all up just as the two ambulances came blaring into the motel's parking area. The deputy still standing, pulled his dead companion out of the doorway so that the medics could see to the wounded man.

The four medics soon had him patched up with a big pad and on a stretcher and into one of the ambulances and raced off to the hospital leaving the others to load the dead ones into the remaining ambulance.

Tom and the sheriff watched as they were loaded and taken away, the sheriff still holding the bag of money.

'Who's going to pay for the damage and cleaning up of the room?' Tom asked.

'Claim on your insurance, Tom,' the sheriff said.

'Will there be any reward for saving that?' he asked, indicating the bag of money.

'That we'll have to wait and see, Tom, but thanks for the call. You did a fine job and I'm sure you'll get something. Pity we lost Eric though. His wife's gonna take this hard. Come on,' he said to his remaining deputy, 'let's get back to the office and count this lot and let the bank know we've recovered their money. There's also the report to write out and check up on poor Joe.' They walked off and left Tom to survey the damage and mess they had caused and left behind for him to sort out.

'I'm not cleaning up all that blood,' Mrs Towser said who'd now come up to Tom and peered once again into the room.

'I'll get the blood cleaned up and the sheets taken away, Mrs Towser, but I will still expect you to clean the place after I've changed the carpet too.' He pushed her out of the way so that he could shut the door and lock it and sent her off to finish the other cabins.

Tom went back to the office cursing at the damage and what he was going to have to do to replace the carpet and mirrors as well as replace the bed linen. It wasn't until he sat down and began to work out how much this was going to cost that he remembered about the second holdall and realised that he'd told the police of only one, but that there was another inside the closet.

He waited anxiously for Mrs Towser to finish and go home and as soon as she had left, he went to the cabin and retrieved the other holdall, glad that he'd got to it before the police came back for whatever reason. He didn't go to the office with it but into his own cabin and locked the door behind him before he emptied the contents of the bag onto his bed. He gave out a low whistle at the pile of money there and sat down on the edge and began to count it.

It took him half an hour to do this and came up with a total of twenty four thousand, six hundred and forty two dollars, all in used bills.

Well they can shoot up every cabin if this is the pay off, he said to himself, but he would still put in a claim for the insurance for it would look strange if he didn't.

Later that afternoon he was visited by the press and had his photograph taken and some were taken of the motel as well though he didn't let them take any of where the shooting took place. It was late before everybody finally disappeared and Tom was too tired to go round looking into the bedrooms and so finished off reading Caroline's letter, which didn't amount to much, there only being two pages left.

The incident was on the front page of the city newspaper the next day and Tom and the motel got a good write up about helping to catch the bank robbers, which was as good an advertisement than could be bought. He later began to get bookings from the city because of this which made for a full motel which was good business. It was still early and Tom got a surprise by Sheriff Rivers walking into the office.

'Morning, Tom,' he'd said to which Tom said the same back. 'We counted the money yesterday and totalled it to just over seventeen thousand. But just between you and me, it was really nineteen but we took a couple to give to Eric's family.' Plus a few more thousand to share out yourselves, Tom said to himself. 'The bank, when we told them, said that there was more than double that taken, so I've come back to look. Have you cleaned the room yet?'

'No. I haven't had a chance yet. I was going to start today,' Tom replied, thinking of the other holdall locked up in his room.

'Has anyone else been in there?'

'No. It's been locked up ever since you left.'

'Well, let's go and look then, plus we want to take the car.' They both trooped out of the office and another deputy, the other survivor from the day before, followed them to the cabin which Tom unlocked and they went in. The place still smelt of blood and cordite and so Tom opened the window as the other two went through the closet, checked the dressing table, under the bed and the bathroom, but no more bags.

The sheriff then went through the clothes that the couple had worn that were still on one of the chairs and he found the keys to the car. The trunk was opened but only held the spare tyre and jack and there was nothing else inside the car.

'We'll take the car away for it might be hidden in the panels or else there was someone else who has the rest. Okay, Tom, thanks for your help. Can you drop in the office later and make a statement, just for the record?' the sheriff asked.

'Sure, no problem,' Tom said as he watched the sheriff walk back to his car while the deputy got into the bank robber's car and drove it out of the motel. This meant that Tom couldn't bank the money but would just have to keep it in his room and spend it as and when he wanted to.

After breakfast, Tom cleared out the bloodstained linen for dumping and manhandled the furniture about so that he could get the carpet up for there was no point in trying to clean all the shards of glass and bloodstains from that either. It was fortunate that he still had some rolls left which he could use. He ordered two more wall mirrors, asking that they be delivered as soon as possible. He didn't do any more to the cabin that day for he got Mrs Towser to watch the office for him while he went into town to the sheriff's office and there dictated his statement of events, omitting of course about observing them and the second holdall.

He also called in at his solicitor's office that had heard of the fracas and asked him to contact his insurance people to send someone down pronto to assess the damage. This he did immediately and got the reply that a man would come down from the city in the next day or two. With all that done, Tom went back to the motel and thanked Mrs Towser for staying on and let her go off home. Visitors soon were booking in and it was still early in the evening when he lit up the no vacancy sign. He made his rounds of the linen lockers but found very little that looked as though it might be worth watching that evening and so he made himself a light dinner and watched some television which was really a rare thing for him to do. He stayed in his room till about eleven before getting undressed and putting on some dark clothing and going out of his cabin and into the trees.

He bypassed the house of Miss Thrush and went to see what was happening at the house of the Stanislavs. Rudolf worked nights in the garage on the corner and his wife Violet, quite often went out in the evening to a disco and usually came back with some man in tow. He was not to be disappointed.

He could see that a light was on in her bedroom and he silently padded across the lawn till he was up to the window and getting there, propped his arm up on the sill and could see the whole of the room through a generous gap in the curtains.

She had just stepped out of her dress and draped it over a chair and was now peeling down her tights which she threw onto her dress. Her long legs tapered from firm thighs down swelling calves to thin narrow ankles. Her dark bush could clearly be seen through the flimsy material of the white panties that she was wearing. Her waist was slim and gave emphasis to her heavy breasts that stood out firm in the small bra of the same material as that of her panties.

She was a good looking woman and knew it as she tossed her head to make her hair billow out and settle on her shoulders. Glancing into the mirror of the dressing table, she gave her hair a gentle push with her fingers and putting a sensual smile on her face, called out, which Tom could hear quite clearly.

'You can come in now,' she called as she draped herself across the bed in what she thought would be as seductive as Cleopatra would have been before receiving Mark Anthony.

The young man she had picked up entered the room, pausing in the doorway to see her lush body spread out on the bed before him. He was about eighteen years of age, well-built and well-endowed it seemed to Tom, the tailored trousers showing the effect that Violet had desired in the setting of her pose.

'Don't just stand there,' pouted Violet. 'Come and make love to me,' holding out her arms. The young man swallowed and entered the room, closing the door behind him. He pulled off his T shirt and dropped it on the floor as he kicked off his shoes. The belt was undone next for him to pull down his jeans, his shorts bulging as he freed his feet. Then the shorts came down and his erection sprang free, swollen and throbbing and swaying in front of him as he stood upright at the foot of the bed. Tom's penis was now throbbing and he pulled it out of his own trousers as he watched the scene being played out.

'That's what I like to see,' Violet purred. 'Bring it closer to me.'

He knelt on the bed astride her as her hands reached up to his waist, suddenly pulling him forward so that he fell on top of her. She rolled over so that he went onto his back as she grasped his prick and bent down and took the fiery pulsing head into her mouth. Her head began bobbing up and down, letting her saliva run down the shaft and into his pubic hairs. She gave out little moans as she drooled on him, her hand coming up to work on him in the opposite direction to her mouth. He squirmed under her ministrations as her other hand began to gently massage his balls in a squeezing motion. His hands were clenched tight down at his sides as she fiercely sucked on him.

'Gently,' he pleaded through gritted teeth. 'I don't want to come too soon.'

She lifted her head up off his prick, now a glistening purple from the engorged blood pulsating round it and her tongue traced around the line of his foreskin.

'You taste lovely,' she said as she released him to sit up and reach behind her to unclip her bra and pull it off. Her large breasts swung into view and then cupped them in her hands, squeezed and brought them together.

'Do you like them?' she asked as his hands came up and rubbed the hard nipples that she offered to him.

'Yes, they're lovely,' as she took her hands away for him to manipulate before he pulled her down so that he could suck on one of the nipples. As he did so, Violet squirmed about, wriggling herself out of her panties before pulling her tit from his mouth and rolling over onto her back and opening her legs.

'Now,' she hissed frantically, 'quick! Fuck me now. I want that cock of yours inside me,' as she began to vigorously rub her clit.

Tom, outside in the garden, was now pumping his hand up and down on his own prick with an ever increasing rhythm, not letting his gaze stray from the scene within.

The young man was now astride Violet, his prick still gleaming wetly, red and hot as her hand took hold of it and guided it into herself. Her legs went up and around his waist as he ground himself deep inside her, her arms holding his shoulders tightly. His hands went under and up to hold her shoulders and pull her down onto him as he pumped away, his balls making wet smacking sounds as they bounced off her bum. He pounded away very fast and went into quick spasmodic jerks as he came inside her.

Tom was disappointed. He had been keeping in time with the two on the bed, so now he had to pump faster on his own hot cock in his hand, until with a small groan, shot his load up the wall of the house. He'd thought that the young man would have had more stamina and last much longer than he had. Wiping himself with his handkerchief, he continued his peeping because he knew that Violet was not finished, even if her friend had for the time being.

The young man lay on his back, apparently exhausted, and Violet took his limp penis into her mouth again, holding it between her teeth as she shook her head from side to side like a dog worrying a bone. Then took it all in, and Tom could see it being moved about by her tongue, and could almost feel the sensation that the young man was getting, so much so that his own prick was rising up again.

She then swivelled round, keeping a firm grip on the cock in her mouth as she swung a leg over his shoulder and leant on her elbows, and Tom, for just a brief moment, could see her wet vagina, the lips red and the soft pinkness of the inside. Her tits were just brushing the belly below her as she gave that prick the wash of its life as the young man's head rose up to lick into her softness.

Tom still watched, but he was not really seeing them as his mind drifted off to the big man who had been with Violet a couple of years ago, just before he went off for the military. Great big thing he was and covered all over with hair from his shoulders down to his ankles like a huge bear, and his big hairless cock jutting out from his fur.

He was strong too. He'd stood there naked with his big erection sticking out before him as she undressed, and her eyes had not strayed from looking at it while she stripped. Her wonderful tits swung heavily when free from her bra as she bent to slip off her panties. Still bending, she had moved forward, her mouth open to take in the head of that fighting cock, which was all that she could manage.

He had laughed and put his hands under her armpits and lifted her up off the floor. Her mouth came off his cock with a loud sucking noise and she squealed as he held her high. She got the idea of what he wanted, and swung her legs round his waist as he lowered her down onto his throbbing erection. She gasped as the head of it entered her and gave out a scream and went taut as he let her own weight ram herself tight up inside her. Her legs came down as she went rigid, impaled on his thick pole, her head flung back and her fingers digging into his shoulders.

Tom watched each of them shudder as she was lifted up by this bear of a man and thumped back down onto his cock. She hung onto his shoulders as she was bounced up and down, her head twisting back and forth, gasping with pain and pleasure at this impaling. Tom was pumping at his own organ but couldn't last as long as the bear. He came in shuddering bursts up the wall, gasping just like Violet was.

Tom watched for another half hour before the bear did finally come. He and Violet had been in several positions on the bed and it was when he was standing next to the bed. She had her mouth on him as she knelt on the bed when he said he was about to come. She nodded, not taking her mouth off him, but he had other ideas as he took a handful of her hair and pulled her head back off him. This made her neck arch and she had her mouth open wide as he worked his cock with the other hand and tried to direct the stream of semen into it. The milky fluid shot out in bursts from the purple glistening head of his prick, most of it missing its target because of his jerking fist. Her cheeks, chin and nose were dripping with it and her tongue was waving about to catch what she could. As the last dribbles were coming out, she forced her head back down to lick these last drops from the fiery head of his cock.

Tom had had to leave the window at this point as a neighbour had turned on their garden light and it was prudent for him to withdraw and not be seen.

He had hoped that this night it would have been the same man, as it had been an excellent performance to watch. The young man in there now seemed a lame duck in comparison, but give the fellow his due, he was ready for another go. Her mouth manipulation to his limp prick had brought it back up to another state of firmness.

She lifted herself off of him and he dropped his head back onto the bed, his lips and chin all wet. He started taking deep breaths as she swung herself round and astride him, her knees on the bed and held his erection upright as she lowered herself down onto it. With his prick and her vagina all wet, she slid down on him quite easily until she was sitting on his upper thighs.

Then she began her movements on him, giving a twist to her hips as she went down, bringing out groans from him every time she landed. Her breasts jigged up and down as she moved till his hands came up and grasped them, squeezing and kneading them as he did so. She flung her head back and gasped with the growing excitement that she felt building up. The rhythm getting faster as she neared her climax with him beginning to arch his back, quivering and bucking beneath her. He went rigid except for his hips as he came inside her and she ground her hips down onto him as she came too, the coming of them both clearly to be seen oozing out and down into his crotch.

Tom came again for the second time, adding more stains to the clapboard wall, watching them climax and her begin to fall forward onto her man, her hair cascading out over his face. Tom wiped himself clean before putting himself away, and then left Violet and her young man exhausted on the bed.

It was the next afternoon that the insurance man came to the motel and inspected the devastated cabin, the bed linen and carpet and took his notes and told Tom that he could then see to putting the room to rights though it was still a week later before the glass mirrored cabin was available once again for a paying guest.

LOVE MOTEL had been open now for nearly five months and it never seemed to be empty and he had started to get people coming back time after time for the special cabins, like the two sisters. They had recommended the place for which he was grateful, not only for their custom, but it made for good viewing. It wasn't hard work in running the place and he was quite happy at the way things were turning out. When all the guests had departed, if they all left early enough, which they had this morning, for a change, he went down to the diner for his breakfast instead of cooking his own.

He was served by the big buxom waitress that had been to the motel for the night twice so far. Though he doubted if she ever remembered getting there, because both times she had been pissed as a coot. The first time was with one man, the next, she had two men in tow.

Tom sat eating his meal that she had smilingly served up to him and he remembered that last time she had been there. It had been nearly three weeks ago and as usual, had been drunk as had been the two men, though it was the soberest one that had come into the office to check in. Tom didn't think they'd appreciate one of the special cabins so they had cabin number ten.

He waited a short while before going to have a look as he hadn't seen her perform on her previous visit. He slipped into the locker and drew back the curtain and saw that they hadn't got very far. She, and one of the men had fallen over and they were all laughing hysterically as the man struggled to get her to her feet while the other was trying to get her coat off as he got up.

She pushed him back onto the floor as her coat came off and the man threw it into the corner. She staggered upright and into the standing man's arms and they both fell onto the bed and bounced back onto the floor and started laughing again. They eventually sorted themselves out and one man pulled a bottle from his coat and uncorked it and put it on the side and went into the bathroom and returned with three glasses. He splashed rather than poured some drink into the glasses and they all had a drink before she got up and picked up her coat and hung it in the closet. The fact that she missed the hanging rail and the whole thing fell to the bottom of the closet went un-noticed as she shut the door. She then delved into her bag and pulled out a small radio and tuned it into a station that was playing some soft dance music. She swayed drunkenly in front of the two men now seated on the bed.

'I'm gonna dance for you,' she slurred. 'Make yourselves comfortable. Take those coats and ties off 'cause you'll choke otherwise.' They peeled off their jackets and ties as she started to sway in time to the music, getting lost in the rhythm. With head tilted back, eyes closed, she began to really move, her arms going up behind her neck to undo the top of her dress. Her hand then brought the dress down off one shoulder as she swayed to reveal the flesh of her upper arm as she pulled it free. This bared arm went across her ample bosom as she did the same to the other arm.

She kept in time to the music as she slowly pulled the dress down as she moved till it fell to her ankles and stepped out of it in front of one of the men. She planted her feet firmly on the floor as she stood with her legs astride and with her hands on her hips, gyrated her big backside with the crotch of her panties just a few inches away from one man's nose. The uncut hairs of her pubics could be seen peeking out from either side of this thin material.

The man made a grab for her, but she swayed back out of reach as she laughed. Then with her feet still again but swaying her upper torso from the hips, reached behind her back and unclipped her bra. This she slowly pulled off so that her ample breasts swung free and from side to side as she swayed. She threw the bra at the other man who caught and sniffed at one of the cups with a drunken leer before tossing it to one side. She kicked her shoes off and slid her hands into the sides of her panties as one man took off his shirt and the other pulled his erection free from his trousers.

He began to slowly masturbate as she slid the panties down, turning to show them the big moons of her backside. She quickly dropped them and turned to face them, feet wide apart so that they could clearly see the biggest sex hole in town vibrate as she stamped her foot in time to the music. With her arms flung wide, she thrust her hips forward and grinned at them as the dance came to a finish.

They put their drinks down to clap her and then quickly picked them up again to empty them down their throats. One got up to go and refill his glass while the other one made a grab for her. She pushed him back saying that she hadn't finished yet and grabbed the nearly empty bottle from the other man and took a healthy slug before she placed it on the hard backed chair that was there in the room.

'Watch now and see the disappearing bottle,' she slurred as she got astride the chair and placed herself above the bottle. She held the neck of this bottle as she settled the top between the lips of her sex. She raised her arms and then began to move her body from side to side as she slowly sank down onto the bottle.

Down she went and the two men and Tom watched as it slowly disappeared. She kept moving down until it could no longer be seen and she was seated on the chair. They both clapped wildly as she got up and waddled over to them and asked one of them to pull it out. He had to use both hands just to get a grip on the base of it and then slowly pull it out of her. It came out with a slurping noise and he then lifted it up to his lips and drained what drink was left in it.

She had meanwhile, fallen over the man who had his cock out, kissing him, his trousers now down round his ankles, hindering his movements. The drinking man dropped the empty bottle and quickly pulled his trousers off, his erection sticking out to the fore. He rolled her off the other fellow and as her legs opened, he moved in and was soon stuck up in her. He fumbled with her tits, trying to suck on a big nipple as he humped her, his toes digging into the carpet to give him more leverage as he pounded away. His partner had managed to untangle his feet and get his trousers off and said plaintively that he was supposed to have had first base.

'Never mind, honey,' she gasped as the other man grunted on top of her. 'Bring your pecker round this side and let me taste it.'

She craned her head sideways as he scrambled on the bed and leaned across her as best he could so that she could take him into her mouth. She gurgled as her lips closed over it and she managed to free one arm so that she could fondle his balls at the same time. The man on top of her shuddered as he came, spending himself inside her and let his full weight fall upon her. She had to let the prick go from her mouth so that she could heave the one that had finished, off of her. The other, with his wet, fiery headed cock was soon taking his place and bucking away in her for all he was worth.

Tom smiled at her as she poured him his second cup of coffee and she gave him a sweet smile back in return. She just ate men. She had kept them two going all night and they were like walking zombies the next morning when they checked out. She took them in, chewed them up and when there was nothing left, spat them out. It would be some time before these two would be ready for another session with her.

Tom paid for his breakfast and thanked her, and she said in turn that it was a pleasure to serve him and if there was anything else he would like, she'd be only too happy to be of service. He politely thanked her and said that he would remember that.

Back at the motel, he did his usual chores of helping the cleaner and supplying her with fresh linen for the cabins. The laundry van had also been and taken away the dirty things and leave the clean ones behind. After a snack lunch, he went and had a short afternoon's nap. He fixed himself a light meal for dinner in the office kitchen and by the time he had finished it, all the cabins had been booked for the night.

Cabin two had been booked a few days earlier because with the rack folded up into the wall as well as the standard bed, it gave space for some of the men from the town to have a private film show. Kenneth Banks, a business man, travelled quite a lot in the course of his work, and whenever he visited Hamburg, always bought several reels of film to bring back home. So that night's booking was for them to see the latest ones he had picked up. Tom knew how many would be coming and got spare chairs into the room as well as a couple of cases of beer and glasses. He had three large trays of sandwiches delivered from the diner and these were put in the room along with plenty of ashtrays.

It was about seven o'clock when they started to arrive, Joe Fields being the first with the film projector, screen and speakers. Ken Banks was next with the reels of films followed by the others in a very short time. So there were eight men crowded into cabin two amid laughter and some shouting, another reason for using that particular cabin as the noise they made would be contained inside due to the sound proofing. Beer cans were punctured and the room soon filled up with the haze of cigarette smoke. It took a little time for them to get settled down while the projector was set up. The screen fell over twice before they managed to get it to stand up on its own against the bathroom wall. Ken Banks told them that he had got one full length film that was not exactly hard core porn, but was worth watching. The other reels were of the hard stuff that would be shown afterwards. This brought out of cries of 'Bring on the action.' 'Give us cock and cunt first,' greeted this announcement, but it was to be the longer film first.

Tom stayed in the cabin, but by the door in case he had to suddenly leave. The film had an English speaking soundtrack to it and the men in the cabin quietened down and settled themselves to watch it. Tom had taken a quick look outside to see that all was quiet and missed the title of the film but noted that the screenplay was based on a novel by Amy Redek.

It opened up to see a girl and a boy finishing a picnic next to a motorcycle and they were wearing the leathers for it. Their dialogue told you that she was a rich girl and he was a bum and they had run off together. But the veneer of their adventure was wearing thin as they had little food and little money left. They packed up the picnic things and rode off on the bike to be overtaken, very dangerously by a swerving car that proceeded to career off the road ahead of them. They stopped and helped the drunken driver to get the car back on the road who, without any thanks, got back behind the wheel and drove off.

They followed him and watched him turn off into the grounds of a large house, narrowly missing the gate posts as he did so. They too turned in to see where he went, but couldn't see where he had gone, but carried on and stopped by a small cottage in the grounds. They got off the bike and he said that he was going to see if anyone was in the cottage, leaving her by the bike. He went up the path but instead of knocking at the door, looked in the big window off to the left. It was a lounge or parlour he was looking into, but didn't notice the furnishings because his eyes fell on a naked man and woman on the carpet. The man's arse was going up and down between the woman's legs as he was fucking her. He could clearly hear the grunting and groans as they really made a meal of it and he could see the woman's face quite clearly but they never noticed him watching them.

The boy went back to the bike, not telling the girl what he had seen, and they mounted the bike and rode off towards the big house that was now visible. They also saw the car parked outside and pulled up next to it as the young driver was still sitting inside. He got out as they stopped and demanded to know what they wanted. The bike boy told him that all they wanted was some food and money or they would tell his father at how being drunk, he had crashed the car.

This was being debated when the man and the woman from the cottage came up to the house and asked what was going on. The bike boy was quick to say that he was an old school chum and had been passing by with his sister and was accepting the invitation to stay for a few days. The car driver stuttered some words out that made it clear that the woman was his mother and the man, a friend of the family.

The bike boy then asked if he could have a private word with the woman and indicated the stable block, with a puzzled look on her face, agreed. So they walked the short distance to the stables and he went into an empty horse stall and she followed him in.

'Well what do you want?' she demanded of him.

'You for a start,' he said, undoing the belt of his trousers. 'I watched you and your friend having a fuck in the cottage. I know he's not your husband, so if I don't get a piece of the action, I will probably tell him.' She called him a filthy little blackmailer as he pulled off his trousers, but stopped when she saw the size of his cock standing out in front of him and started to take her dress off. She was a lovely looking dish and looked even better without her clothes on.

The men in cabin two cheered as the biker pushed her down onto the straw and buried his cock inside her. There were no close ups but you could see his cock ramming in and out of her but you did get a close up of her face and tits as she was being fucked and evidently beginning to enjoy it. They both gave out cries as they came together, her with an orgasm and him coming inside her.

They went back to the house where the others had gone inside and found that they could stay for a few days. The girl had guessed what had happened in the stables and the boy told her to shut her mouth as they were staying there to get what they could out of the place. At dinner, the film's dialogue told them that the woman's husband was an inventor and was just putting the finishing touches to his formula for a new type of fuel that was far cheaper then benzene. Also present at the table was his secretary, the friend of the family as well as the son, mother, biker and girlfriend.

After dinner, the biker cornered the mother in one of the halls and got her into a bedroom where they stripped off and you had another viewing session of them fucking each other. Then it was back to the girlfriend's room where you see her strip naked and see that she's got tit's the size of balloons. At this, the biker turns up and quickly takes his clothes off to see that he's rampant again and after her sucking on it for a little while, he gets down to fucking her.

Next morning, he asks the secretary if she would drive him down to the local town so that he could order a part for his motorcycle as it couldn't be ridden. She was about thirty years of age, wearing a somewhat shapeless dress and her hair done up in a severe bun. To make her look even plainer, she also wore glasses that had thick rims that made her eyes appear larger than they actually were. She agreed to this as she had the time and drove him to a local garage. While inside, he phoned somebody, the film didn't reveal to whom he spoke, but he said about this fuel formula and was promised a fantastic amount of money if he could get his hands on it.

On returning to the car, he invited the secretary to lunch for doing him this little service of driving him about. She agreed and so they had a pleasant meal. When it came to paying the bill, he found that he'd left his wallet behind at the house and if she would pay it, he would reimburse her later. So she paid and they then drove back to the house.

It was after dinner, and the secretary was in bed reading when after a knock at the door, the biker boy entered to give her the money for lunch. He sat down on the side of her bed and here, the dialogue was terrible and the poor author must have cringed at the way they mangled that scene. That she might look beautiful without the glasses and her hair down etc, to which he pulled out the pins for it to cascade down to her shoulders and on taking her glasses off, he kissed her.

The scene then changed to them both being bollock naked and fucking themselves silly. Her breasts were as large as the mother's and after sucking on them, she goes down and sucks on his erect cock. This time you did get some close ups of them in the sixty nine position as she sucked and he licked.

Then he's back in his room and the girl friend is going down on him, really sucking and deep throating him and then as her nose has been into his pubic hairs, tells him that he's been fucking some other woman for she can smell the scent. He pushed her off and told her to either go fuck the other men or go fuck herself. He was laying the groundwork to get hold of the fuel formula and make them both some money.

The next day he bedded both the wife and the secretary as the girl friend gets fucked by both the son and the friend in a threesome session. The film actually showed her having the son flat on his back with his cock up her vagina as she lay on top of him and the friend fucking her up the arse at the same time.

There were claps and cheers at this scene from the men in the crowded cabin.

Later, the girl friend is having it off with the son who professes to have fallen in love with her and wants her to ditch the biker and stay with him. She decides to stay and tells him of the biker's plans and so they go to see his father. He's already guessed what was in the wind for he knew that the boy was fucking his secretary and so tells them of what he'd planned to do about it. Here, the girl announces that her father was a very rich man and she was sure would finance the processing of his fuel idea.

The scenes inter-shifts here with the father telling of what he proposed to do and then to the boy as he's fucking the secretary about how to steal the formula and she agreed on being promised a half share of what they would get from selling it.

The son and girl go off to fuck each other as the father prepares the final draft of the formula for the secretary to type, which she does, not knowing it to be false. Another scene shows the family friend fiddling about with the motorcycle before it cuts back to the biker and the secretary in bed and as he's humping her again, she tells him that she has the formula and that they can leave at any time.

It's early evening and we see the biker and the secretary getting onto the motorcycle and driving off away from the house. It follows them for a minute until, with some close ups of the bike's front wheel, we suddenly see this wheel disintegrate and both are thrown onto the busy highway where they both get hit by various other vehicles, obviously killing them. Then it's back to the dining room of the house where the father raises his glass in a toast to the new fuel and, with a wink to his son and the girl, the possible merger of the two families.

There were lots of groans from the men in the cabin as the film came to its end.

'Not enough cunt,' someone called out. 'Throw it back.' another called out, with other catcalls being made at the film's end.

While the film reels were being changed, more beer cans were opened and Tom did the same to the cabin door to let out some of the smoke and get some fresh air into the room. He also went out and checked that all was okay round the motel during this reel changing period and was back as one of the hard core porno films began. There wasn't any dialogue, just a mish mash of music as a background to the first film. The colour was bad as was the story line, of which there really wasn't one.

It opened to show a man and a woman in the grass kissing before they started to strip off each other's clothes. He is a European and she looks like an Eurasian. Brown body, small tits but a wide gash. The man is soon tonguing her and we see that they are being watched from behind some bushes by another female. She is fingering herself as she watches the girl start to suck on the man's cock. Many close ups of all the private parts are shown as her fingers play with her own clitoris as the other girl licks the head of the rampant cock held in her hand. Then the girl in the bushes is grabbed from behind and her top is pulled down as she kneels there. This action reveals a pair of massive tits that swing loose and are then massaged by a pair of hands. Her dress is then thrown up to reveal a shiny wet vagina and the man's cock sliding up inside her. The film kept flipping backwards and forwards between the cock sliding in and out of one woman as the other sucks and tongues the cock of the other man.

Tom noted that many of the men there had their own cocks out and were slowly masturbating as they watched the film, handkerchiefs to the ready as they worked on themselves. When the woman in the film brought the man to the point of ejaculation, she held it clear of her mouth so that you could see his sperm shoot out for her to catch it in her mouth. Tom saw that one of the audience, so engrossed in the film, came and missed his handkerchief and shot his load onto the back of the man in front. Better him than the carpet, thought Tom, who would have to had it cleaned up later.

It was all very well for them to watch these films and get their rocks off this way, but it wasn't for Tom. He could see it live in the flesh and in full Technicolor and didn't need this kind of stimulation, so he slipped out of the cabin into the fresh air and decided, though he had got an erection from watching the films, wanted to do it to himself in one of his own private viewing rooms.

He heard the claps and cheering faintly when this film finished and they were into the second film when he went back inside the cabin.

Two naked girls, up on the screen, were playing about in a pool by some woods when the scene cut to a field. There was already one tent up, assuming it was that of the girls, because two boys erected another one quite close to it. The next scene showed you the boys in a bar having drinks and then it was back to the girls as they came out of the water. Naked and displaying their wet tits as well as their fannies as they put on a minimum of clothing before going into their tent.

Then they are naked again, kissing each other before performing cunnilingus on each other, close ups of tongues licking and sucking at the clits and vaginas. Back to the bar as the boys, evidently a bit drunk, leave and make their way back to their tent. One stops off for a piss while the other crawls into the tent. This first one, when finished, stumbles on and falls over a guy rope and begins to crawl into the wrong tent. He doesn't notice the girls in the dark as he strips off and promptly falls asleep. The girls are giggling and as one lights the lantern, the other pulls off the boy's covering to reveal a flaccid penis.

Close up of one girl taking it into her mouth and bringing it up to a full erection and then giving him a hand job as she sucks on him further. She holds it clear of her mouth as he comes so that it could clearly be seen leaving the eye of his cock and splattering her face and mouth. She smiles as it sprays over her, licking what she can and was just taking it back into her mouth when the film started to go all brown and a white spot began in the centre and quickly moved outwards as the film burnt out.

Loud groans and catcalls as the projector was stopped and the lights turned on for them to repair the film. The room erupted into talk and Tom decided that he'd had enough of it so he slipped back out into the fresh air. He walked around for a bit to clear his head after all that smoke and thought it was about time for him to inspect the other cabins from the linen lockers.

He checked each one of his private viewing windows to see what the occupants were up to. In most, the activity was nil and the last one to be checked was cabin number one. Earlier that evening, with all the cabins booked, he was surprised that it had been a month since this couple had last used it. He hadn't recalled the name when it was booked over the phone but recognised her as soon as she had walked into the office. A very well dressed woman of about thirty five, precisely spoken, in fact, so much so that it marked her up as being a foreigner. Her companion was the same small slim Eurasia girl of around the early twenties in age. This was their fourth time here, coming in once a month since they had heard of cabin number one. Tom had only watched them the once and thought it was time that he saw the show again that they put on.

He went into that locker and as usual, took care to lock the door behind him before moving over to the window and drawing back the curtain. The older well dressed woman was always referred to by the other younger one as Lady, and still looked elegant, though attired completely different to what she had been wearing when booking in. She was now wearing calf length boots of soft leather that had high heels. The high heels made her calves swell and gave her legs an impression of being of great length. Her thighs were bare up to the tight black pants that she wore, but they were only pants in the sense that they were round her thighs and waist. There wasn't a crotch piece to them so front and rear were clearly visible. Her waist was quite narrow and had full heavy breasts which were encased in a black leather bra with the centre pieces missing so that her nipples showed through. It was strapless, leaving shoulders and neck bare as was the lower half of her face, the upper part being masked. This covered the top of her head and down to the cheek bones and across the bridge of her nose. The eye holes were large and they made her own eyes seem twice their normal size.

In her hand she carried a whip, the handle of which was large and thick and tapered off to end with five strands of chamois leather. These strands she kept wet. Lady was overdressed in comparison to the little Eurasian girl who was completely naked and Lady referred to her as Minty. They were using the ceiling hooks this night and Minty's wrists were in a loop of silken rope that were through the hooks so that her arms were apart and high above her head. She was not suspended as her feet were flat on the floor but it stretched her taut in front of her captor.

Lady was talking softly to Minty and gently flicking her with the whip. So gently that just the barest whisper of sound reached Tom as the fine ends caressed the slim dark body. The gentle swish as they moved lazily through the air and landing with a sound like quiet rasp of a painter's brush upon canvas as the tips of the thongs moved across the small pert breasts. Minty moaned as their ends touched her flesh, not from pain, but pleasure. Lady was not a true sadist as Minty was a masochist. Tom chuckled to himself as he remembered an old joke.

"Beat me," begged the masochist.

"No," gloated the sadist.

Minty kept twisting her fine body to catch the whip on different parts of her body. A fine film of perspiration lay between her breasts and around her trimmed pubic hairs. Lady, as she used the whip with a deftly practised hand, was using the other hand to alternately touch and rub her now rigid nipples and rub herself through the open front of her pants. With Lady crooning softly and Minty giving out small groans, the motions of both of them increased. The whip moved faster, Minty twisted more and Lady rubbed herself vigorously until Minty cried out.

'Now, Lady, now!' Minty, her head thrown back and with her hands tied high, stood with her legs as far apart as she could get them as Lady went down onto her knees between them. Minty's hands now grasped the silken ropes tied to her wrists as Lady lifted the stretched legs and put them across her shoulders as she moved and pulled Minty's wet cunt to her open waiting mouth. As the mouth went inside the outer lips and the tongue started to lick inside the inner ones, Minty shuddered and began to work her body violently against Lady's face.

Lady had a firm grasp on the hips and held tight as she worked her head in between the ripe young thighs. It was the same pattern as before, Tom noted. There was little variation in what they did.

When Lady had finished between Minty's thighs, both had obviously had an orgasm, stood up, her face and lips glistening with

Minty's juices. The same kind of juices that Tom noted were slowly moving down Lady's own inner thighs. These Minty would be licking later when untied, but for now, Lady began to lick the salty perspiration from Minty's taut stomach. Then as Minty's feet fell back to the floor, Lady carried on licking upwards and between the small breasts and over them as they shone in the light. Tom played with himself and dumped his ball sac contents as usual over the wall in front of him. He was not ashamed of his cock for it was of average length but thicker than most. This was probably due to the fact that he'd used his hands daily on it for many years past now, then more than once a day if he could get some good peeping in.

He left Lady flicking Minty again with the whip, building up into another sucking climax He knew that the names they used for one another was from the fact that Lady was addressed so was because she dressed and acted like one and that he'd heard Lady refer to the other girl as her bint with the hole, hence Minty.

He left the locker and them two still at it and went over to the office and let himself in and opened a beer and waited for the film show to finish which wasn't that long. He stood on the boardwalk and said goodnight to those leaving, the last being Ken Banks who came and shook Tom's hand and thanked him for getting the beer and sandwiches in and paid him for them and the room before going off himself. Tom went over and locked the cabin and decided to clean the place up in the morning before turning in himself.

IT WAS late afternoon when a big burly black guy entered the office.

'Have you got a room for me and my girl?' He asked.

'Only one left,' Tom replied. 'It's not the usual motel room and it costs a little extra.' Tom was referring to the cabin with fur.

'Can I see it?' the man asked.

'Sure,' Tom said, taking the key off its hook and led the way across the yard. He'd noted the smartly creased shirt and trousers. 'Army?' he asked.

'Marines. Staff sergeant, on furlough,' the man replied as Tom opened the door to cabin five and showed him the room.

'Gee, that looks great! She's gonna love this pad,' he said. 'We'll take it.'

'If you'll just sign the register,' Tom said giving him the key and they walked back to the office. Tom watched him sign in as Amos Fletcher and took the money. He watched him walk out to the car.

'It's a great pad, Andy,' he said as he got into the car.

Andy? thought Tom. A strange name for a young white girl that was in the car, then he twigged with his name being Amos, from a television show. Tom decided to get a better look at her and so gathered up some towels and walked across to the locker as Amos got Andy out of the car. She was young-looking and white as already mentioned, and Amos scooped her up into his arms as Tom opened the locker door and went inside.

'Now close your eyes until I say open them.' Amos said and then entered the cabin carrying the girl in his arms. He shut the door easily with his foot and turned on the light, carrying her as if she was weightless. 'Now keep your eyes closed and kick off your shoes first.' She did as she was told and wiggled her feet till her shoes came off, her eyes still screwed shut. 'Now I'm putting you down on the floor, but keep them little eyes closed and tell me what you can feel with your toes.' He lowered her gently till she stood on the floor.

'I'm standing on a bearskin rug. It's all furry.'

'Well, open your eyes now and have a good look,' Amos said. She opened her eyes and looked at the floor, the bed, the walls and the chair and exclaimed, 'Fur! It's all fur.' She sank to the floor and squirmed about, rubbing her face against the floor covering. 'Ooooh,' she purred, 'and it's all fur me,' she said, making a pun of the word. Amos laughed and pulled her upright without any effort.

'Do you like it?'

'I adore it,' and flung her arms round his neck and pulled his head down and gave him a big kiss on the lips. Amos pulled free.

'I bet your mansion hasn't got a bedroom like this,' he said.

'We haven't got a mansion, it's just a house in Baton Rouge, I keep telling you,' she pouted.

'A house with twenty bedrooms is a mansion to me, honey,' Amos said, 'and with your plantation.'

'It's not a plantation. It's a cotton mill,' she interrupted.

'An' those fiel' han's out ev'ry morn' pickin' cotton fer daddy's mill,' Amos laughed.

'Stop it, Amos,' she laughed.' Daddy's only got the mill and he employs whites as well in the mill, and on equal terms.' Amos picked her up in his arms and looked her in the face, all serious now.

'And you've never been to bed with a black man before?'

She dropped her eyes and whispered, 'No. I…I've been too scared to. Daddy would've killed me.'

Amos carried her to the bed and he sat down with her on his lap. He lifted up her chin with a finger and looked into her eyes.

'Are you sure you want to with me?' he asked.

She held her head up and looked into his face, 'Yes,' she whispered, 'I do.' He leaned forward and kissed her lightly on the forehead and she gave out a sigh and nestled her face into his shoulder. He stroked the back of her head as he spoke.

'Honey. Did you ever see a black man without his clothes on?'

She nodded and lifted her head.

'Once. They caught a nig…a black that had tried to rape a white woman. They stripped and flogged him. I didn't think it was very nice what they did.' They were silent for a moment before she lifted her head up and laughed, 'And stop introducing me as Andy.' He laughed with her and the serious mood was broken. He whispered into her ear,

'Is my white Southern chicken ready to be fried?'

'Your little Southern chicken is going to fry your balls off if we don't hit the sack,' she retorted. He laughed and stood her up in front of him. She pushed his hands away and undid the buttons of his shirt and peeled it off of him. His black chest gleamed like coal that's been washed from the coal face. She dropped it on the floor and undid the front buttons of her blouse, pulling it free from the waist and took it off and dropped it onto his shirt, her short skirt suddenly falling to the floor round her feet. Because of her height, her breasts looked large but were small and firm as they came into view as the bra also fell to the floor. Well rounded with the nipples hard with her inner excitement and stood before him with just her panties left.

He slowly reached out his hand and completely covered one breast and felt her fast heart beat for a moment or two before letting his hand drop. She then eased off her white panties until they too fell at her feet. Her belly was flat and her mound was prominent with its covering of fine hair.

'Off to bed, you grinning ape,' she laughed, 'and let me try it for size.' He stood, towering over her, his power showing at his crotch. 'Big boy,' she whispered, pressing her hand against it for a moment. He stood aside and she sprang onto the bed, rolled over onto her back and slowly wiggled about. 'My God, this is sensational,' she said as she squirmed back and forth. Amos had shucked off his shoes and now dropped his trousers and his pants and stepped free from them. She saw his weapon with his ball bag hanging below.

'Wow! That's beautiful,' she said. 'Let's open up the church because I'm gonna play that organ tonight.' She settled herself in the middle of the bed. 'There's a Southern belle here that needs ringing for I want to hear them balls make me clang.' She held out her hand. 'Come here, you big black bastard, and fuck me. I would just love my daddy to see this big black buck climb across his sweet little daughter and screw the arse off her.' Amos knelt on the bed next to her and saw that her eyes were alight with some inner hatred. She took his prick in her hand and held it fast. 'I want to be fucked and fucked, pumped and bored by this, Amos.' He put his hand between her thighs and found her sopping wet, her juices already flowing and he gently rubbed her clitoris. 'Amos, fuck me. Stuff me now. Do it all. I want the lot. Everything, everything. Now Amos, now!' she screamed from between gritted teeth. He swung across and mounted her. With her juices lubricating the way, he went straight in right up to the hilt and she gagged.

'Oh God! God, God, God, ooooooh.'

Amos plunged in and out as her hands clawed his back, leaving red weals where she scratched him. Her heels began to drum on the bed as she bucked up to meet him as he drove in and out. She came shatteringly and had her legs clamped to his hips like limpets and kept on digging her fingers into his shoulders. He banged away with his balls smacking loudly in the juice that ran down between the cheeks of her arse. As she climaxed for the second time, his hands went under her shoulders and he lifted her clear off the bed and rammed her down on his shaft as he sent his load high up into her womb. Her head fell back and she ceased moving, just a twitch as he gently lowered her down onto the bed again. Her face was covered in sweat as were her breasts which Amos now gently stroked with his free hand.

Tom had been in a frenzy watching them and had been so excited that he came long before they did and was pleased for himself and them as it had been that good.

She opened her eyes and smiled up at him. 'You lovely big black fucker you,' she said and closed her eyes again and purred. She stretched out as best as she could underneath him. 'It still feels big inside. Are you ready for more?'

'You lovely bit of white meat. Of course I'm ready for more,' and he started riding her again, more slowly this time, with deep thrusts followed by short ones, almost withdrawing the head of his cock out of her as the vagina squeezed to stop him from pulling out completely as they rode together slowly. They had all night to ride.

Tom relaxed as it would take him a little time to be ready for more. He went out of the locker and had a quick check round the grounds of the motel to see that all was okay before returning to the locker. He was in time to see her come running out from the bathroom laughing, with Amos chasing her with a towel in his hand. She dived for the bed as he whipped her with the towel across her bum. She yelped and lay sprawled face down on the bed and rubbed her backside.

'That stings,' she moaned.

'Stings?' he cried. 'You damn well nearly cut my pecker off,' rubbing his big black erection.

'Did it really hurt?' she asked.

'Damn right it did,' he said. She bounced up onto her knees and held out her arms.

'Well, come here and let me kiss it better.'

He walked over to the side of the bed, his prick swaying ponderously from side to side as he moved. She grabbed it with both hands and pulled him closer to the bed. She looked down at his black tool with its large pink head half showing from its foreskin. She gently moved her hands, making the foreskin slide back and forth from the head.

'It's big and lovely,' she said and bent her head and took him into her mouth. That was all she could get in, the head. He stood firm while she moved her head back and forth, working her tongue round it inside her mouth. Her hands kept moving up and down his prick, occasionally pulling his balls up as well. Amos gently pried her loose and her head away from him, his prick making a sucking plop as it was reluctantly let free from her mouth.

'Let's both get some pleasure instead of one,' he said as he stretched himself out on the bed.

'Weren't you getting any pleasure out of that, for I certainly was,' she said. 'Mmmmm,' she mouthed as she took him back into her mouth as she moved her body round and straddled him. Her knees either side of his head, her small tits gently brushing the lower end of his rib cage. His hands slid down and cupped them both completely and slowly kneaded them. She gave out a moan and shifted her hips so that her open sex lips went down closer to his face. He then buried his face and sucked on her with his mouth.

They pleasured one another this way for some time as small moans and sighs filled the room. She released his cock from her mouth and gently nibbled her way down the underside of his shaft to his ball sac and then took one of his balls into her mouth and rolled it around like a plum. She did take both in but was unable to do anything with them for they filled her mouth completely, so she released them and chewed her way back up his rampant black cock to the pulsating fiery red head. Pulling the foreskin back as far as she could, she then worked her tongue round the sensitive part where it joined the flesh, the G string as it's known.

His teeth had been nibbling at her now inflamed clitoris and his tongue had excited the inner membrane of her vagina, so she pulled free and rolled off of him, panting.

'Stay still,' she said throatily. 'I'm ready to ride.'

She swung herself round and went up onto her knees and steadied herself above the outstanding example of prime manhood that he was now holding erect for her, the big black cock of Amos. Her hand took over as she guided herself down onto the head and then grimaced as she forced the large head of his cock inside and then let go as she slowly began to sink down on it. He moved slightly and she froze.

'Don't move, you bastard,' she hissed. 'This hurts till I'm ready.' With her head held back, her clenched teeth could be seen through her partly open lips. With her arms tensed, her hands flat on her upper thighs, she slowly went down. The big black prick of Amos could be seen to disappear slowly, inch by inch to be swallowed up past the lips of her sex. She came to rest on his thighs with the whole length embedded deep within her and her held breath now whistled out between her teeth.

'Man!' she breathed, 'you sure have got some cock there.'

Her limbs relaxed now and she grinned down at him. He grinned back at her, his hands cupped behind his head so that he could see her properly as she had sat down on his prick.

'Missy,' he chuckled, 'that sure is a tight warm glove that you've put on my lil ol' pecker.' She gave a little bounce. He grimaced and grabbed her hips with his big hands. 'Steady, ma balls ain't made of stone.' She laughed and reached behind and underneath her and grabbed them and slowly rubbed them.

'They sure do feel like stones.' She let go of him and placed both hands flat on his stomach and started lifting her arse up and down, very slowly, only a few inches at a time. 'This reminds me of when I lost my cherry,' she said, still slowly moving up and down on the black stalk. 'It was a big black horse, same colour as you. It nearly split me in half just sitting astride of it. I had my feet hooked in the stirrups and was only holding him on a loose rein when something startled him. He took off like the wind.' Her movements on top of Amos started increasing. 'He flew across the fields with me, having lost the reins, just hanging onto his mane. Every time my arse hit the saddle I felt that I was cutting myself in two. I was wearing white riding pants and with the pain, I felt I was getting wet. I could see that the crotch of my pants was being stained red. Following the pain came the excitement. I'd played with myself before but that was nothing compared to what I was feeling then.' She was moving up and down a little faster now. 'The feeling inside of me was getting bigger and bigger as the horse raced along. He then jumped a small ditch and as we landed with a thump on the other side, my fanny bored into that saddle and I poured my lot out into my pants. Blood and come made a sticky mess that I bounced around in. I was delirious with the pain in between my thighs coupled with the wondrous burning relief that I felt deep inside of me. I laid forward in the saddle and rubbed myself as hard as I could and met the rising saddle with my mound.' Her hand was now rubbing her Mount of Venus as she went up and down faster. Amos' prick was still rock hard and her juices could be seen smearing it and running down into the hair round his balls. She moved faster, her breath coming in gasps.

'I lost count of how many times I came and lost some of my senses too, because when the horse baulked at a large fence, I wasn't aware of it and lost contact with both horse and saddle. I just knew that the whole shit was knocked out of me when I hit the ground. I exploded inside as well, just like I'm gonna do in a minute.' She was going into a frenzy. Plunging up and down, waving her head from side to side as she pumped herself on top of Amos. He started to meet her by raising his hips, grinding up and squashing her sex lips in a splatter of juices. He held her fast as she bucketed about as she orgasmed and her coming poured out, mixing with that of his that he was jetting up into her at the same time. She suddenly then went limp and fell forward onto his chest and his arms went round and he gently rocked her.

Tom cleaned himself down after fisting his prick in time to them, shooting his load as usual all over the wall. He had taken his trousers off this time before he started and when he was cleaned up, put them back on.

They had separated when he looked again through the window and she had just started to caress the limp tool between Amos' thighs.

'It's all messy,' she said. 'Let me clean it up.' She rolled down and using her tongue, started to wash him just as you see a cat do to itself. She gave out little moans as she ran her tongue down the length of his prick and spoke in between licks. 'I wish my daddy could see me now. He'd die of a fit. His sweet little girl, licking and sucking this big black cock, mmmm.' She gave him a playful nip with her teeth. 'I wish we had a camera. I'd take a picture of me doing this and send it to him. No! Even better.' She bounced up onto her knees and squatted back on to her heels. She leaned forward earnestly towards Amos who lay back contentedly. 'What I would like,' she said continued, 'is to have a photograph taken with you stuck right up inside me. Another man, also black, stuck in me from behind, and a third, black too, standing in front of me and I would be sucking his prick. Have a big mouthful of it and then another man playing with my tits,' she rubbed hers to illustrate, 'while two more jerked off and their seed splattering all over my body.' Her eyes were alight with the vision she'd conjured up, her mouth bearing a grim smile.

'You shore hate your daddy, don't you,' drawled Amos.

'I hate the bastard's guts,' she said fiercely. 'Him that was always preaching to me. Telling me how he was going to marry me off to a fine Southern gentleman. He'd bring one of these fine Southern gentlemen home who would be as old as he was. They'd get blind drunk and then he would leave me with this fine example of chivalry saying that it was his kind of Southern hospitality, and off he'd go to fuck his little black wench. While I then would have to fight these old men every time. My clothes were usually torn to shreds and I would sometimes catch a black eye when they raped me. But daddy got his cotton mill in the end. What did I get? Days in bed recovering and one visit to the doctor for an abortion.' Her shoulders shook as she started to cry and Amos pulled her down and nestled her in the crook of his arm. His big black hand soothingly caressing her bare back as she sobbed into his neck. 'I only managed to get away from him a few days ago,' she got out between sobs.

'How did you manage that?' Amos asked softly. 'You'll feel better with it all spoken. I'm a good listener.' Her sobbing slowed and she moved in closer to him and pulled his hand up to a breast and moved it around so that he was rubbing it slowly as she spoke.

'It was about five days ago now, I think,' she sniffed and moved the back of her hand across her eyes, wiping the tears away. 'I was in the kitchen when the grocery boy came. He was a young Negro, about my age.' She glanced up at him shyly. He smiled down at her as she continued. 'Well, he was just about to put the groceries on the table as the bag split. Some of the things fell onto the floor and we both bent down to pick them up at the same time and banged our heads together. I fell backwards onto the floor myself and as I did so, my dress came up to near my hips and you could see my panties. I lay there rubbing my head and laughing. The boy rubbed his head and started to apologise and began laughing too. He knelt down to help me up. The trouble was that he'd knelt between my open legs and was just reaching forward when daddy came into the kitchen. I can imagine what it looked like. Me lying there with my skirt up to my waist and the boy down there already between my legs. Christ! The bloody noise he made.

'You dirty no-good fucking black bastard, trying to fuck my daughter in my house.' He grabbed up something and belted that poor boy right round the head. He fell over me and daddy kept hitting him as the boy tried to get away from the blows. I was there, trying to struggle my own way out from underneath. The boy's knee was on my skirt and it tore as I pulled away and it came off. Then daddy made a grab for the boy but caught my shirt instead. Such force he was using, ripped it right off my back. I wasn't wearing a bra for it was too hot then, besides, I don't need one, do I?'

She gave Amos' hand a squeeze that was still rubbing away at her tit. 'They stand up alright without support. Well I was knocked flat onto my back again as the boy fell once more, though this time, his face was now down between my tits and daddy went berserk. He near killed the boy, kicking him out of the house. The boy fell down the steps with daddy shouting rape after him as I struggled up to my feet. Well I was up on my feet when daddy came back into the kitchen. His face was bright red, his hair all over the place.'

'You...you...you whore!' he shouted at me. I had one arm across my breasts and was trying to pick up my skirt when he hit me. I went flying backwards into the hall and I quickly got up and tried to run as he came chasing out after me and tried to grab me. His hand only hooked into my panties and of course, as I moved forward, they tore and he had them in his hand and I was now naked. I ran into the lounge with him chasing me but there was no way out of there so I had to turn and face him as he came through the door.

'No black bugger's going to touch my daughter,' he growled and I shouted back at him, still trying to cover myself.

'What about all those white buggers you let rape me?' I cried. 'He hit me again then and I fell backwards onto the rug.' She rubbed her hand across the fur covering of the bed they were lying on. 'It felt like this but much coarser. His shirt had been ripped in the kitchen struggles and I now saw a strange look on his face as he looked at me lying naked there on the floor. I know now what it was, it was lust. For two years now he had been giving me to men who could help him get what he wanted and it was just then that he saw exactly what he had been giving away. He tore the rest of his shirt off and pulled the belt free from his trousers. He came and stood over me waving this belt.

'Don't ever let me see you looking at another nigger and never let another of those black bastards into my house again.' Then he hit me. He belted and belted me with that leather strap. It was fortunate that he was so angry that he hit the carpet most of the time, but all of a sudden, he was on top of me.

'He tried to put his thing on me. He was stronger, but I fought him like crazy. I was going frantic. My own father! How could he do this? My arm went back and caught the cord of the table lamp. I pulled it off the table onto the floor and picked it up and bashed it onto the back of his head. As he cried out and jerked up, I hit him again and caught him clear round the side of his head this time, just above his ear. He went out like a light. I managed to get upstairs, resolved to running away. I threw a few things into a grip and went back downstairs. I looked into the lounge to see if I had killed him. Fat, white and lifeless he looked but he was still breathing.

'I think I could have killed him and gotten away with it, but I then had a brilliant idea. So I went back up to his room and collected all of his clothes that I could find. Even those that he had been wearing. I took them all out into the back garden and dropped them on the ground and took the lid off the cess pit and kicked the lot down into it. I didn't leave one stitch of male clothing in the house, nor any of my dressing gowns or nighties. I even went back in and ripped out the telephone wires, picked up my bag and fucked off to the bus station in town.

'I changed directions about three times and about six different buses before I met you in the diner. I'm glad that I stopped there for I liked the look of you the moment you walked in. I would have died if you hadn't spoken to me, but you did and now here we are.' She sat up and rubbed her hand across his chest as she gave him a smile which he returned as his hand came up and began to caress a breast. They looked like they were ready for another session for Amos was rising up fast.

Tom wasn't ready for any more so he pulled the curtain across the window saying, 'Fuck away, Amos, it's all yours.' He locked the door of the locker and walked across to his own cabin and was soon in bed and asleep.

THINGS HAD quietened down now and Tom hadn't had any reason to call on the sheriff for some time now. The motel was quite established and there were not many nights when it wasn't fully booked, and this day was no exception. He'd had a restless night which was usually a sign that something different was going to happen and he just hoped that it would be something good and not a disaster.

It was in good spirits that he carried out his daily chores and by the early evening, had rented out all but one cabin. This was soon to be taken for he had a phone call from a man wanting to rent a room and Tom was only too glad to say yes. He hadn't asked for any specific cabin but all that was available was the leather one, number three. Tom could hear that from where the man was phoning that there was a party in progress and so assumed that the man wanted an excuse to leave early so he got the cabin.

It was then about eight o'clock and Tom, after switching on the no vacancy sign, fixed himself a light meal in the small kitchen at the back of the office. Though this had been designed originally as a cabin, it was now the office with some slight changes. No bed for a start or dressing table closet or bedside tables, but a counter a few feet in from the door. Behind this was a table that doubled up as a desk and a filing cabinet. The bath-room hadn't been installed for it had been made into a small kitchen and instead of a door off to one side, it had a big open archway in the centre. So when standing at the desk, you could see the sink at the back and the window that had a venetian blind instead of a curtain.

But every first Saturday of the month, the office became a small poker room. The school, well it was a proper school during the day, but in the evenings, it became a college of evening classes for advanced pupils. It was some of the teachers, well four to be precise, that booked Tom's office, for their game of cards.

Tom's desk, dining table, became, when it was turned over, a card table for the underside had been covered with green felt. He brought in extra chairs and even laid on some light snacks and some booze in the kitchen for them. It was more than poker they played some nights. They sometimes got one of the female students to come over to make the sandwiches and serve them with their drinks after they had got started and Tom wondered if they would have one of them over this coming night. He got the table and chairs sorted out, the makings for the sandwiches and plenty of ice.

Just after he had finished, the teachers and professors arrived. First there was Mr Alberts. His subject was history and he looked as though he was part of it as well. About fifty years of age, short and quite thin with not much hair on his head, but had blue twinkling eyes that still had the sparkle of youth.

Styles was a professor of English, around forty and short like Alberts but quite fat and gave a very jovial showing as to how Friar Tuck of Robin Hood fame must have appeared. A large round face with three chins, no neck to speak of and a body that looked almost round. All he lacked was the tonsured pate and cassock. Professor Jenkins was a rather morose looking sobersides of a man that taught Math. Tall as Styles was short and thin as the other was fat. His head was square as was his chin and he was all angles, just as though he'd been made up from the subject he taught. He even wore square rimmed pinze nez glasses to finish off the effect and did indeed look his forty years. The odd man of the group was Mr James. A youngster by comparison to the others, only being twenty eight years of age. An average looking man that would pass un-noticed in a crowded room of three people. Crew cut style hair but sombre old fashioned clothes.

Tom had put out cards, chips etc, and as well as beer in the fridge, there were three bottles of Scotch in the kitchen with the tray and glasses. The players after saying their hellos to Tom, mixed themselves their first drink and sat down to play cards. Tom left them to their game and took out with him the key to the last cabin that had been booked over the phone. He wouldn't then have to interrupt the game when the last guest arrived.

Tom had just reached his own cabin door when a car pulled into the lot and parked. Tom started to go to the car but the man was quickly out and met him before he got too close to it, but he'd already made out the fact that there were two people still in the car. The man took the key and thrust some money into Tom's hand and said that he would sign the book in the morning. Tom shrugged his shoulders and while the man returned to the car, moved towards his own cabin but then changed his mind for he wanted to see who exactly was going to be in cabin number three.

He was settled comfortably in the locker with the curtain drawn back when the cabin door opened and two young women about twenty five years of age and the man, around the same age, entered the cabin. No baggage was carried in with them, Tom noted. The women just carried their purses. The man had evidently been told about the motel before, because he fetched three glasses from the bathroom and knew where the small supply of liquor was kept as all the special cabins had. He took off his jacket and poured out drinks for them all as the women were making appreciative noises about the cabin's décor being all done over in leather. The man slumped into one of the soft leather chairs with his drink and the two women sat on the leather covered bed and sipped at their drinks.

'What a drag that party was,' the man said. He was looking at the woman to the right. 'I said to Joan before we left home that I hoped that we would see a friendly face there tonight.' The other woman nodded and Tom noticed that this nodding woman wore a wedding ring on her left hand and he looked at the other woman's hand to see she wasn't wearing one.

'I'm glad you were there, Ann,' Joan said. 'Though we've only spoken a few times before, you seemed to be the one friendly face in that sea of strangers. The noise and the heat, and John said, Ann looks lost here as well. Ask her if she'd like to get away for a quiet drink somewhere else.'

'Well I'm glad that you rescued me from that old fogie,' Ann laughed. 'I couldn't stand him. I'd gone with Julie but she got latched on to one man's arm and looked like clinging there all night.' They finished their drinks and John got up and refilled the glasses. Joan stood up too and shrugged off her jacket and threw it on the bed.

'I'm going into the bathroom to freshen up. Would you like to come too?' she asked of Ann. She nodded and took off her short bolero style jacket and picked up her small bag and followed Joan into the bathroom.

Tom sensed something and shot along to the other curtain and pulled it open and viewed into the bathroom. Both of the women had opened their bags and Joan had just finished washing her face and was gently applying some fresh make-up, very lightly. Ann was washing and as she dried her face and hands she said, 'When you said that we would go somewhere for a quiet drink, I didn't think it would be in a motel room.'

'Oh, we always do that,' replied Joan, dabbing her lips with a tissue. 'When we go out to a party we always stay at a motel for the night. We have a baby sitter that sleeps over at the house as we don't like creeping in at sometimes five o'clock in the morning. We'd rather have the rest of the night to ourselves and go home at a decent time in the morning. The baby sitter gets the breakfast and all that. It works out fine.' Ann was doing her face at the big mirror, looking straight into Tom's eyes though she couldn't see him. Joan kept up a rattling conversation, 'Now don't be shocked, but confidentially, John said to me at the last party we saw you at, now there's a lovely young woman. She could talk intelligently, didn't get drunk and had a wonderful figure and it was one woman that he wouldn't push out of bed. He said that, really. I laughed at him and it made me envious of you.' Ann had coloured up a bit.

'You shouldn't be envious of me,' she replied. 'You've got a perfect figure yourself and have great beauty as well.'

'Well, John was struck by you and that's why he asked if you'd like to come for a drink with us, and I wanted you to come as well.'

They finished doing their faces and went back into the bedroom. Tom caught John speaking to them as he pulled the curtain closed on the bathroom window.

'Well have you been chewing over your mutual friends at the party?' Tom moved back to the bedroom curtain and pulled it aside and looked into the room. They were talking and drinking and the conversation slowly worked its way round to sex as Tom guessed it would eventually. They talked of the erotic arts, the Chinese prints, the Karma Sutra and other forms of sexual literature. John's tie and shoes were off. Joan was curled up on the lower end of the bed and Ann was propped up on the leather pillows.

Joan stretched herself out across the bed and yawned, her blouse tightened across her chest and they could all see that she was not wearing a bra for the nipples were firmly outlined through the thin material. She sat up and put one of her hands over one of Ann's as she looked at her face.

'Well I think it's time for bed.' Her voice went softer as she continued. 'Would you like to join us? Please don't be offended but John has said that he would like you to share our bed and I would too. I think it would be a wonderful way of us really getting to know one another. As I said, please don't be offended by our offer for neither would we be if you said no. John would drive you home and we could forget these last few minutes, but I myself would like you to say yes.' She gave Ann's hand a gentle squeeze. Ann, slightly red in the face, had obviously expected some kind of proposal, looked down.

'I…I…don't know what to say,' and she gave a little laugh. 'I should…well I feel a little flattered but…well…I…,' she gave a quick nervous laugh. She tossed her head so that her hair swung about her face. 'Oh hell, why not,' she smiled. 'I like both of you very much, but I...I...er, haven't...I don't know...,' her voice trailed off.

'Don't worry, Ann darling,' Joan said soothingly. 'Neither have I before.'

John, who had been gazing about the room with that air of abstract boredom that plainly showed he waited desperately for the answer to be yes. He beamed at them both now and silently raised his glass and toasted the two women. Ann saw the gesture and raised her glass with a shy smile and Joan picked hers up with a grin and drank. John got up and turned off the main light, leaving on one small glowing lamp by the bed.

'Make yourselves comfortable, girls, while I have a wash,' he said and went into the bathroom and closed the door. Joan left the bed and started undressing and draped her clothes over the back of a chair, just leaving on her brief panties.

'Come, Ann,' she said. 'Don't be shy now. I'm sure you've got a perfect figure. One to be proud of.' Ann gave a nervous laugh and swung off the bed and quickly shed her clothes, leaving her panties on as Joan had.

'You've got a much better body than I have,' Joan said admiringly. 'Look. My legs are stumpy compared to yours and your tummy's flatter than mine. And just look at these breasts! They droop so, not as fine looking as yours are.'

To Tom they both looked the same and were really very nice to look at and they both also had good figures. Joan was making Ann feel better and more confident by her chatter.

'And just look at my bush,' Joan said as she slid her panties down. 'All tangled again. I trim it regular but it still looks like a wild garden.' Ann now slipped down her panties and stepped out of them.

'You look perfect in all ways, Ann,' exclaimed Joan and took her hand. 'Come look,' and opened the closet door right back so that they could both see themselves in the full length mirror fixed to the inside of the door. 'You look just divine.'

While they were partially out of sight of the bathroom with the closet door open, John emerged just wearing his shorts. He pulled back the bed covers and dropped his shorts, his erect cock bouncing high as it came free, and got into bed and made himself comfortable in the middle. The two women turned and stepped towards the bed and John gave out a low whistle and Ann coloured again as his eyes roved over her body.

'Hasn't she got the most perfect figure, John? Better than mine,' said Joan. He sat up in bed and held a hand to each of them. Ann tentatively took his proffered hand as Joan took the other and they walked round to their respective sides of the bed as he pulled them towards him. Joan climbed in one side of John and Ann slid in on the other. Her face coloured more when the covers were lifted for to get in properly and saw his erection hard and lying up on his stomach. Ann pulled the covers up but it wouldn't come far enough up to cover her breasts.

'Ann, you look wonderful,' John said.

Joan leaned across his shoulder and said softly to Ann, 'John is very gentle and understanding.'

John looked at Ann as she lay full length in the bed, the cover only coming up as far as her midriff. Her breasts were very firm and the nipples were red and rigid and she had a hesitant look on her face as John looked at them.

'Kiss me, Ann,' he said very softly and bent his head towards her. Her arms tentatively went up to his neck and she closed her eyes as they kissed. He kissed her gently and passionately and made it a long kiss before their lips parted, her eyes now open wide.

'He kisses well,' Joan said from the other side of the bed having watched them. Ann pulled his head down for another kiss and this time her body moved as they did so. John's hand went to her breast and with his palm, gently rubbed the taut nipple with a circular motion. He moved slightly to her side and slowly pressed the other breast tighter to his chest and his hand then moved down her body, pushing the bed cover at the same time so that his fingers could be seen weaving their way through her fine pubic hair. The hand came to a stop on her mound but the fingers had moved out of sight but they could be seen to move as he pushed them between her thighs. The kiss held as she opened her legs and his fingers slipped inside the wet lips and gently probed the vagina and clitoris.

She broke off the kiss with a gasp for breath, beads of perspiration on her forehead and between her breasts for his hand was still moving inside her and she was becoming aroused. Her hand went down and grasped his erect prick and held it firmly as she squeezed and moved her hand up and down on his shaft.

John's head went down and his mouth was firm on her breast as he sucked and nibbled on the nipple and she gasped again as his hand began to move faster and she too began to move hers the same. He swung a knee across her leg and forced her legs to open wider as Joan eased off the bed cover further down for more freedom of movement as John now lifted himself in between Ann's now open legs. He paused for a moment looking down at Ann and as he lowered himself down towards her, Joan took hold of his erection and with her other hand, opened the lips to Ann's sex and guided John's tool inside.

Ann had stiffened at the feel of the extra hand touching her but relaxed as she felt the head of his cock enter her wetness and begin its slide up into her. She grunted as his full weight descended on her and her arms went up round his neck as he levered himself up onto his elbows but with them now joined together from the waist down. He smiled down at her and she smiled back as he began to move and she moved too in time to his rhythm. His cock was sliding in and out of her, giving her some exquisite pleasure and felt Joan's hands begin to caress her breasts and could hear her crooning about how wonderful her tits were. Ann gave herself up completely to the erotic sensations that she felt. It was with grunts and cries of pleasure that they both had their orgasm at the same time, him shooting his load up inside as hers were released to mingle with his.

John knew she had come because of the increase of slipperiness of the inside of her tight little cunt that held his prick so firm. She knew his load had entered her by the sudden increase of size of his cock head of the prick embedded deep inside her as well as the small shudders he gave along with his grunting.

Joan was rubbing herself between her thighs as she rubbed Ann's tit and though she didn't climax, she was wet enough and now ready for anything. John finished his shafting of Ann with a few quick strokes and then pulled out and rolled off of her and laid his head down onto one breast. She gave out a little cry as he withdrew and as he laid his head down on her, she gently stroked the back of his head, her eyes closed and a dreamy expression on her face.

'I hope you two haven't forgotten that I'm still here?' Joan asked. Ann's eyes flew open, her face colouring again for she had forgotten in the excitement of her orgasm. John lifted his head off Ann's tits and smiled at Joan as he rolled off the bed and stood up and gave himself a stretch. His dick was now limp hanging between his legs and he walked over to his clothes and found a cigarette and lit it.

'You're no good for me now, are you?' Joan said.

'Give me a few minutes and I will be,' he grinned back at her. She pouted her mouth at him and turned on her side and looked at Ann.

'How was it?' queried Joan. 'He was gentle, wasn't he?' Ann nodded dreamily.

'It was so nice, so nice,' she murmured. 'I haven't felt so...so...satisfied for such a long time.' She nestled back contentedly.

'That's two out of three satisfied so far,' Joan said. 'I've got to wait.' She placed her hand tentatively on Ann's flat stomach. 'May I touch you, Ann?' she asked. 'I've never touched another woman before.'

'Neither have I,' Ann murmured as she nodded her head. Joan moved her hands up and cupped one breast.

'Your body is so firm and smooth,' she said as she rubbed the breast more and shifted her body over the short space between them till their bodies were touching. 'May I kiss you?'

Ann with her eyes open now, nodded and met Joan's lips with her own and they kissed fiercely and passionately. Their bodies moved tighter together as John sat and watched them through half closed eyes as the smoke curled up from his mouth. Joan rolled back to the middle of the bed pulling Ann on top of her, their lips still glued together as they continued the kiss. Their breasts were flattened out against each other and their legs entwined as they brought their mounds together and started rubbing them against each other. Ann broke free from the kiss and arched her back high and Joan's head came up and her mouth fastened hungrily on one of Ann's breasts and they rocked like this for several minutes before Joan fell back, panting.

'Can I show you what John does to me sometimes?' she asked. Ann fell forward and nodded and she rolled off Joan who swung herself round on the bed and opened Ann's thighs with her hands and buried her mouth into Ann's cunt. Ann gasped and put the edge of her hand into her mouth and writhed at the touch of Joan, not with disgust but with pleasure and gave out a loud purring noise past the edge of her hand. Joan sucked and bit, tongued and probed and did more to Ann than what John had ever done to her. She lifted her head after several minutes and grinned back at Ann.

'That's what I try and get him to do, but he's only a man and it's very difficult to explain exactly how it should be done. Did you like it?'

'Like it?' exclaimed Ann, 'it's...it's...oh, do it again,' she pleaded.

'Will you do it to me at the same time?' Joan asked. For an answer, Ann started to lift Joan's leg across her and Joan helped and straddled her and bent her head down again into Ann's box. The classic sixty nine position. John watched them, life slowly coming back to his prick on watching this performance. Tom also watching, was bashing his meat again. Both the women bucked and writhed on the bed and gave themselves up to the mutual delight and both rocketed out their orgasms and cleaned each other as they came. Then sated, Joan rolled over and they both lay there gasping like fish out of water, head to tail on the bed. John now stood up and clapped his hands in applause.

'Wonderful,' he said. 'Wonderful. But I think you forgot that I was still here. Can I join the party?' Joan gestured weakly.

'Climb aboard the sex express,' she said.

'And have fun on the ride,' finished Ann. Joan turned round on the bed and John climbed in between them again.

'As much as I enjoyed watching you two beautiful girls having fun, it was still too quick for me to rise again,' John said. With a mischievous grin, Joan sat up.

'I know how to raise the dead,' and she winked at Ann before she lowered her head and took John's semi flaccid prick into her mouth. In its limp state she was able to get her mouth completely over it, her lips pressed right down to the root of his shaft.

'Mmmmm,' she mouthed, breathing through her nose. With his cock stuffed in her mouth, she gave the impression of having a meal as she chewed it. She had to gasp for air as his cock started getting rigid and forcing her to relinquish it bit by bit. Her head was slowly being forced back by his growing tool. First the root was showing and then his prick just seemed to be growing out from between her lips until all she had inside was the head held firmly between her teeth.

He squirmed with both pain and pleasure as her teeth scraped over the uncovered head of his cock. With a sigh she released him completely and his fiery red headed prick stood up for their inspection.

'There,' she retorted. 'I said I'd make the bloody thing rise up.' She bent down again and fastened her teeth to the root of his now rampant cock. 'Come and join me, Ann,' she said through her cock-filled gritted teeth.

'I...I...never...Oh what the hell, there's not much left I haven't done,' Ann said and bent her head to the other side of John's cock and fastened her teeth opposite Joan's. With their noses touching, the two women worked their teeth slowly up his shaft till their lips met at the top of the glowing red beacon that was now throbbing and really pulsating. They kissed with their lower lips resting on the top of his glowing prick.

'Hey you two,' he called. 'It's ready now.'

They broke the kiss and Joan rolled over onto her back and parted her legs for John to swing himself between her thighs as she used her fingers to open wide the lips to her wet sex.

'Now, John,' she panted. 'Now. Fuck me, come on and fuck me now!'

He fell forward holding his prick with one hand to guide it into her and released it as he entered her. He slid down until he was on top of his wife, the full length of his prick inside her now. She started moving first with her hips twisting at the same time as she moved back and forth on the bed, her arms around his back.

'Harder,' she urged him in a fierce whisper. 'Hurt me. Push it harder. Fuck me harder. Harder!'

'Yes, John, harder!' Ann exclaimed who was bouncing on the bed alongside them, as excited as they were. 'Fuck her. Fuck her harder!' Ann's own fingers were well up inside herself, working away and bringing her up to a feverish pitch in her excitement. John strained and strained, ramming himself down harder each time he went forward into Joan. His balls slapping at her arse as he pounded away. Ann's other hand suddenly encircled his balls and followed his movements in and out, cushioning the slap and gently massaging them as he drove his prick as deep as he could into his wife Joan. Ann felt his balls twitch and pump as the hot sperm shot out of them and the hardness of them go softer as they emptied. This actually being able to feel this eruption of seed gave Ann an orgasm, hers coming at the same time as Joan and their noises of their coming mingled in the air. The three of them fell back exhausted on the bed.

Tom cleaned himself up and prepared to leave. He guessed that they would soon revive and start again, but in the meantime, he would go outside to catch his breath and then look in somewhere else. As he closed the curtain he heard Ann speak.

'I'm glad I said yes and stayed.'

'So are we,' one of the others answered.

Tom went out and locked the door behind him and walked up towards the motel's entrance just in time to see a long legged girl turn in at the entrance. Tom moved to meet her and saw that she was a very well stacked young woman. She hesitantly asked Tom if he knew where Professor Alberts was playing cards. She went on to explain that she'd been asked to do the drinks and see to the food for them. Tom felt sorry for her if she didn't know the truth. She was very beautiful and Tom reluctantly escorted her to the door of the office. It was always old Alberts that seemed to find the girls for this job. Tom knocked at the door and ushered her inside. Alberts got up from the table and welcomed her in.

'Come in, Sarah, and meet the team. Thanks, Tom.'

Tom shut the door and went round the back to his peeping spot for the office did not have a locker between it and his cabin. He squeezed between his pick-up and the kitchen window that had this venetian blind that didn't work very well. As this was directly opposite the office, he had a good view of the inside as well as of the kitchen. There was a small window open at the top to let the cigarette smoke out and was also the means to hear all that was spoken inside.

He got to his spot just after the introductions had been made.

'Well that's us,' Alberts was saying. 'You probably knew the faces from the school but now you know the names to fit them to. You'll find all the drinks and the food makings in the kitchen there, so why not rustle up some drinks first and then start to make us something to eat, eh?'

She then walked towards the kitchen, her high heels making her calves swell and her tight arse sway. She was wearing a short flared skirt, low on the hips, and a matching halter top. Her hair was tied up at the back into a pony tail, the length of which came half way down her back. Her arms were bare as were her shoulders, showing to the full a nice golden tan, a very healthy looking girl indeed. She passed into the kitchen and was back almost immediately with a tray and collected the empty glasses, asking each what they wanted to drink before returning to the kitchen.

Styles gave a huge wink at Jenkins and nudged James.

'Alberts sure knows how to pick them, eh?' he chuckled and the card game carried on. The girl, Sarah, served them their drinks and made some sandwiches and passed these around. The men ate them mechanically while playing and she went and sat down in a corner looking bored watching them, filling up a glass when it was empty.

Sometime later and Tom was getting fidgety when a big pot on the table had just been won by Alberts. He sat back flushed with the winning of it with the other's cards being slammed down onto the table at the huge bluff that had won it. Glasses were drained and Alberts called Sarah over.

'This game tonight is getting boring. Let's inject some life into the game.' He winked broadly at the others. 'Sarah. See that pot on the table?' She nodded. 'Half of that could be yours.' It was quite a large one judging by the previous ones. 'How about serving us up the following drinks topless? Like they do in the clubs. Half the pot,' he reminded her. Her tongue came out and nervously licked her lips. She stood a moment in thought, her eyes on the pot in the middle of the table and then nodded.

'Ah, one drink at a time,' said Styles, his three chins nodding.

'Yes,' chorused the others. She nodded with a flush to her face as she collected the empty glasses and went into the kitchen and the men sat back and waited.

Tom shuffled about outside of the kitchen window, waiting to see her reaction. It differed with each girl this first time. She had put the tray down and stood there hesitating for a short time before clearing the tray. She refilled the glasses and put one of them on the tray and poured out an extra whiskey and held this in her hand as she hesitated again. She then knocked this whiskey back and pulled the halter top off over her head.

Her breasts were full inside of the bra and they tautened as she reached behind her back and undid the clips and they suddenly sprang free as the bra came off. Perfectly round, firm and full, they proudly jutted out from her chest, the nipples standing out like pebbles on a beach and they had the same sun tan as the rest of her chest and shoulders. No bikini strap marks of white flesh to be seen. She picked up the tray and walked proudly into the office where the men eagerly awaited her entrance. The men gasped, whistled and cheered as she went as red as a beetroot in the face and leaned across the table to put the glass in front of Jenkins. Her breasts gleamed in the reflected light from the cards and chips on the table.

'Mine next,' said James. 'Beer please, Sarah.'

She retreated to the kitchen and came back with his beer. As she passed it across, his hand reached out to take it and gently brushed one nipple as he did so with the back of his hand.

'Thank you, Sarah,' he said. She returned twice more with the other drinks and again had one tit brushed by a hand as they took their drinks.

The card game was forgotten.

Half of the pot had been pushed aside for her and this was given to her to take back into the kitchen, but at the same time, the first drink for Jenkins had been drunk and he gave her his glass for a refill.

Coats had been taken off when they had first sat down to play but now the ties came off and shirts were unbuttoned and being opened. As she was serving the next round, James took one breast in his hand and kissed it. She didn't stop him but paused a moment, red in the face. At the same moment, Jenkins hand slid up her skirt and gently squeezed her inner thigh

'Sarah,' said Alberts. 'Look, there's only the four of us here. The rest of the pot's yours if you take it all off.' She didn't say anything but returned to the kitchen for the next drink.

Tom watched avidly at this usual ploy of theirs as she poured out the next drink and placed it on the tray and seemed to be contemplating what to do. Evidently the pot on the table was a good enough incentive because she undid the clip at the side of her skirt and it swirled off and she quickly took off her panties. She had a slim waist and perfect hips with good strong and long legs but kept her high heeled shoes on. Her pubic hairs had been trimmed and made a perfect vee of black velvet to compliment the golden tan of her body. She took up the tray and went into the room. There was a stunned silence as she moved into the room and stopped just inside the door. The collective breaths were whistled out at this fine example of womanhood.

'Jesus,' breathed one.

'Kerist,' said another. Then they all tried talking at once as she moved over to the table and put the glass down. She was away again before they could touch her and at the door, she stopped and gave them a bump and grind before she disappeared from their view.

They pounded the table and clapped and cheered as she left the room, but she was back in a moment with another fresh glass.

'Sarah dear,' Alberts said. 'Bring your bag in with you next time.' Styles patted her bare arse as she went past him back to the kitchen. She returned with the last glass and her bag. She put the drink down and Alberts took her bag and opened it and swept the pot inside. He held the bag open still at the table and looked at her before speaking.

'Sarah,' he said. 'You are the most beautiful girl we've ever seen.' Chorus of ayes followed from the others. 'You have shown us a woman. A real woman and we are but men of mortal flesh and blood. We can't stand the sight without being affected by such beauty.' She looked at him and saw that it was true. The front of his trousers had the bulge of his prick showing very prominently. James was rubbing the front of his trousers at the same time.

'You've aroused us to a high pitch of sexual excitement.' He waved his hand towards the table. 'Let me put the rest of what you see on the table into your bag if you would do us the honour of relieving us all of our present distressing conditions.' The table held as much if not more than was already in her bag. She looked at the four grinning men all rubbing themselves and with a flaming face, nodded her acquiescence.

They jumped up from the table and all the chips were swept into her bag and the glasses and cards were cleared from the table. Sarah sat on the edge of the table and then leaned back and spread her length out over it. The men fumbled their clothes off and flung them into all corners of the room. Her pert arse was on the edge of the table and she drew her knees up and placed her heels there also but kept her legs together until all the men were naked as she was and standing round the table looking at her.

James had the better body and looked in good shape. His prick stood out hard and thick, the foreskin stretched back a little from the head that was red and pulsating. Jenkins had a cock like his body, long and thin and curiously bent so that it stood out to one side. Styles fat belly hung over his short fat dick and his breasts were almost as big as hers. Alberts, the oldest one of the group, had a cock that was like a stout pole that sprouted out of his grey bush. He approached her first.

'Sarah. May I have the honour of being the first?' he asked.

'Yes,' she whispered, 'but first could you do something to me? To make me ready for you all?'

'With pleasure, my dear,' he said and she let her legs fall open and her pubic bush parted and the lips to her sex came into view. The bud of her clitoris gleamed wetly at the top of the parted lips. Alberts went down onto his knees and buried his tongue inside the moist pliant flesh. He used his top teeth to lightly scratch at her clit. She moaned as he probed as deep as he could reach with his tongue and after a few minutes of this murmured to him.

'Now, professor, I'm ready. Do it now.' Her eyes were closed and her mouth opened and the tip of her tongue ran over the parted lips. Alberts rose from the floor and without any preamble, drove his prick in deep. She trembled and gripped the sides of the table as he, with rhythmic precision, thrust himself in and out of her. Bringing the head of his cock to the very entrance of her twat before ramming it home again with his balls smacking her taut little arse.

The others hopped about in their excitement awaiting their turn and while Alberts had been down licking her out, they had been cutting the cards as to which order they would take for their turn at delving into the honey pot. She shuddered with Alberts as he thrashed his way to his climax, holding back till it exploded out of his cock while on his deepest thrust. The walls of her vagina contracted of their own volition as he came, holding his prick tight inside her. The sensation of him pulling out seemed to draw her insides out too and she moaned for him to wait but he'd already withdrawn.

She had flung her arm across her eyes but now felt another cock head knocking at her door. She tried to close her legs but they were being held apart.

'Not yet, a few minutes please,' she begged, but she was too late in speaking for the next was already now inside her, not very far but there being pushed in and out very fast.

'Sorry, my dear. I can't hold it much longer, I'm nearly there,' gasped out the fat little Styles. He wasn't either. Seven short quick strokes and he was panting as his sperm shot inside her. He withdrew immediately afterwards having come inside her and she closed her legs and rolled over onto her front.

'A few minutes rest, please,' she asked, but her hips were suddenly pulled and her feet landed flat on the floor. She still had her upper body laid across the table as her legs were moved apart and she felt a finger probe into her anus.

'No!' she wailed. 'Not that, please!' She started to lift her body off the table but a hand in the middle of her back held her there. She felt the finger withdrawn but to be immediately replaced by what she knew to be the prick of Jenkins. Being long and thin, it didn't have any trouble invading this private part of her person. His body met hers as his prick went in to its full length, the tops of his thighs rested momentarily against the cheeks of her arse. This touch electrified him and he took his hand from her back and slid both hands up and firmly grasped her breasts. He held them tight as he fucked her up the rear, using them as handles to pull her closer towards his forward thrusts. Even with her tits being manhandled so roughly as well as being fucked up the arse for the first time, her own body started to respond to this new experience and she began to move back to meet his forward thrusts. But he had already begun to groan and bucking up hard to her body, let loose his load.

This she felt and it inflamed her senses and she cried out as he withdrew his fast becoming limp tool. She fell forward across the table as he let go of her and stumbled away to collapse in a chair. An arm helped her to roll over and the soft voice of James she seemed to hear from a long way off. She could hardly hear him for the roaring in her ears with James still talking.

'Just me left, Sarah. I drew the last card. Please hang on for me.'

He was easing her back up onto the table and she was very pliant in her still shocked state of just being buggered, and rolled where she was put. Her arms listlessly at her sides, her legs hanging down which he lifted and propped them up on the table's edge. Her knees fell wide apart and her soaking wet pussy was clearly to be seen and he quickly stuffed his cock inside her. After watching the other three, his prick was a raging, hot, thick throbbing bar. He worked it inside her being as gentle as he could as he moved in and out of her wet passage, slowly picking up a beat. She responded slowly to this rhythm and her legs came up and over his hips. He was then able to drive deeper with each forward thrust as he fucked and his cock seemed to explode inside her as she began to get close to a climax herself which didn't happen because he pulled out too fast.

She sobbed as he pulled out and she lay there exhausted and was still lying there weeping after the men had got themselves dressed. They gently helped her off the table and into a chair. One of the men went and fetched her clothes from the kitchen and handed them to her and she automatically began to dress herself and her weeping had now really turned into a crying jag and she sobbed and sobbed. The men stood about her looking on helplessly. Tom was now watching this with apprehension. He had come himself twice, sending his seed all over the bushes whilst watching the fucking of Sarah for the girl had the most perfect figure he'd seen in a long time, but now he smelt trouble.

He hurriedly adjusted his clothes and scooted round to the front just as the office door was flung open and the girl came rushing out. She didn't see him and only went as far as his cabin door and she leaned against it, crying. Two of the professors had come out of the office and he could hear one of the others saying something inside.

'……..fucking trouble. That's what's going to happen now.' Tom stopped the two at the doorway.

'I'll see to her,' he said.

'We don't want her to make trouble, Tom,' Professor Alberts said.

'Neither do I,' said Tom. 'I'll handle it. Leave it to me.' He turned and started forward for his cabin and Sarah.

'If there's no fuss, Tom, we'll see you alright,' Alberts called out. Tom approached the girl who flinched when she heard his step behind her.

'Don't be frightened, Miss. My name's Tom Love. I'm the owner of the motel. What's happened? Why are you crying?' He gently put his hand on her shoulder. His hand trembled as he touched her for he could still see her in his mind's eye, the beautiful breast just below that shoulder. Also, it was the first time that he'd actually touched a girl for the past nine years.

'Please hide me,' she sobbed. 'Please hide me.' He opened the door to his cabin and she quickly stumbled inside. Tom followed her in and turned on a small table lamp so that the room was only lit by this soft glow.

He told her to sit down in the chair while he made her a cup of coffee. For this, he had a small electric ring in one corner of the cabin. Her sobs had slowed and he could see and feel the beauty of her in spite of her tear streaked face as he handed her the coffee and asked her to tell him what had happened. Of course he knew exactly what had gone on for hadn't he seen it and shot his load twice while watching. But she calmed down a little after a few sips of her coffee and gave him a short and brief tale of what had happened.

'I thought I was just to serve drinks that I was getting paid for. It was more than I would get babysitting. I wasn't shocked when they suggested that I serve them without my top on, I'm not a prude. Nor really when they asked me to do so without any clothes on. There was so much money there that I got carried away. When they suggested sex for the rest, well....I....I didn't think it would be as bad as it was.' She started sobbing again and Tom passed her a handkerchief and said some soothing words to her and she stopped and continued in a faltering voice. 'I...I it was horrible and they looked revolting.' Tom went and poured her another cup of coffee.

'Go and wash your face,' Tom said indicating the bathroom, 'and make yourself look pretty and you won't feel half so bad. Through there, go on.' He coaxed her out of the chair and she went into the bathroom. Tom sat and pondered as to what to do with her as he waited until she returned into the room.

'My, what a change,' he exclaimed. 'You really are a pretty young woman. Come and sit down again. If you feel as you look, you must be great.' She sat down and gave him a weak smile.

'Thank you very much,' she said in a low voice. 'You've been very kind and I do feel a little better now.'

'Now what are we going to do with you?' queried Tom half to himself. 'It's just gone two in the morning.' She gave out a gasp.

'That late! I can't go sneaking into the hostel at this time of the morning,' she wailed. 'What'll I do?'

'You can stay here for the night,' Tom said gently, 'No,' he said as he held up his hand as she started to protest. 'You'll be quite safe here. I will go and sleep in the office and you can have the bed here.'

'No,' she said. 'One of them might have seen me come in here and come in after you've gone.' Tom laughed.

'No, they will have gone by now.' She looked at him.

'But what about you? You might be like one of them,' she said. Tom laughed at this.

'No my dear, you've got nothing to fear from me. I can't be like them.'

'Why?' she asked. 'Are you queer or something?'

'No, no. Far from it,' Tom chuckled, 'but I haven't, er, touched a woman for about ten years now.'

'Well if you're not queer, how come?' She put a hand to her mouth. 'I'm terribly sorry,' she whispered, 'I didn't mean to be rude asking so personal a question. Did you have an operation or something?' she couldn't help asking.

'No. It was an experience I once had back in the army that, well, I can't do anything when I am with a woman.'

'Tell me,' she said.

'No. It's a long story. You wouldn't want to hear about it.' She gave him a soft coy look.

'It's gone two o'clock you said. I can't go back to the hostel at this time. I can listen. I'll get into the bed and you can tell me, eh?' Tom looked at her thoughtfully and then nodded. 'Well, turn your back then and I'll jump in.' Tom did as he was asked and could hear the rustle of her clothes coming off and he could picture her perfect body sliding in between the sheets. He could feel his prick starting to rise at the thought and when she said he could then turn round, it began to deflate knowing that he wouldn't be able to see her body because she was now in the bed. In the soft glowing light he could just see that her eyes were open even though her face was half in shadow. He pulled the easy chair over closer to the bed and sat down and began to tell her of part of his life in the service of his country.

'I joined the army because I had to,' Tom started, 'and I'm now twenty five years old. I went through training the same as everyone else did and I suppose I was the same as them really. I was not exactly a virgin soldier, but I'd only known one woman,' and he smiled at the thought of Caroline, now the Princess Till-I-Come. 'One night I had been over the wall with some of the boys. That is, we went out of the camp without a pass. This meant sneaking out through the wire and back the same way. Well I'd had too much to drink that night while outside. With a couple of the fellows, we found our way back into the camp but by a different route than the one we left by.

'I stopped for a pee and somehow, lost the others and didn't know what part of the camp I was in. It turned out to be the women's section for I had looked into some of the windows to try and find out exactly where I was.'

This was not strictly true for Tom knew precisely where he was and was taking advantage of having a good peeping session while he was there. He continued with his story.

'Well I looked in and saw all these women in various stages of undress and it got me all excited. So much so that I must have drawn attention to myself.'

And how, Tom thought. Getting his prick out and belting away at it in his drunken state. His belt had come undone and his trousers had fallen to his ankles. In a drunken sway, he tried to keep upright but couldn't move his feet and he'd fallen backwards into some bins with a loud clatter. A window had shot up and a broad with bloody great tits hanging out of her bra leaned out and yelled to the others that there was some bum of a G.I. outside with his fucking pecker in his hand. Go and grab the jerk and grab him they did.

'Well, I fell over and the women came out and jumped on me,' he continued with the tale. 'They dragged me inside their hut. We called the living quarters huts, but they had about thirty beds inside them. Into the middle of the hut they dragged me. I don't know how many of them had a hold of me but I tried to act the gentleman and didn't hit out at them.'

He'd fought them tooth and nail as they had dragged him inside.

'But if I'd known what they were going to do to me in there, I would have gone down fighting like a true marine. Our guys thought that tangling with the gooks in Korea was bad enough. If Uncle Sam had sent those women in, they would have mopped up the whole lot in half the time that it took the men. I was stripped naked and strung up to a beam. Sarah, may I call you that?' She nodded but was becoming so engrossed in his tale that she didn't think as to how he knew her name. 'Sarah, what they did to me defies description. They literally tortured me with their bodies. Of course the first thing that happened to me was to... to...get, er, over excited.'

'Tom,' whispered Sarah from the shadows cast by the lamp. 'I said I'm not a prude. A spade is a spade. You mean you got a hard on. An erection.' He could sense that she had a smile on her face at his present discomfiture.

'Well, er, yes. I got a...a hard on, seeing all those naked and half clothed women made my...my....'

'Prick?' queried Sarah.

'Yes, my…my…prick stood up like a Red Indian's totem pole. They… they…, you don't want to hear about it.'

'Have you ever told anyone else, Tom?' Sarah asked quietly.

'No,' he replied.

'Well tell me then,' she said. 'Get it out of your mind. Go on.'

'Then don't look at me,' Tom said. Sarah shifted fractionally in the bed and he could see her shape under the covers and was a little shocked when he noticed that her hand appeared to be moving in between her legs. Not being able to see her face gave him a little pleasure at seeing her touch herself while he was telling this story about himself. It was usually him that played with himself while he heard other people's sordid stories.

'Well, with my, er, cock out in front of me, they began to bait me. They waved their, er, tits under my nose, put a chair close and step on it and shoved their fannies into my face. They licked my cock, sucked it, bit it, spat on it and hit it. One specialty they had was for one woman to hold me from behind so that I could feel her breasts rubbing my back and her breath on my neck. Another one with enormous tits would come in front of me and trap my pulsating cock between her tits and then jerk me off so that my come would shoot up into her mouth. Then she would hit my erection with her fist until the pain made tears run down my face. They would tickle it and rouse it up again so that they could work me over so that I shot my load again.

'They would call me all kinds of filthy names and hit my prick again. When I was lucky to pass out from the pain, they would revive me again by throwing buckets of water over me till they could do something else. A broom handle was used quite often. First it would be stuck violently up my arse and worked about till I'd bleed, then with this handle, hit my cock again. Pins they stuck into me and other little torments, all the time their hands working on my tool, to raise it up again, to hit and torment me. Again and again they did this for five days. Five days they kept me tied up and tortured, all the time abusing me and my body.

'I was posted A.W.O.L., absent without leave, and when they finally threw me out of their hut without any clothes, I was arrested for indecency while in the women's compound and thrown into the cells. I was never able to touch a woman after that. I tried. After I was released from the cells, nobody would have believed my story if I'd told it, apart from that, I was too ashamed to have told anyone. I tried to go with a woman but it was no use for as soon as I was alone with one, I would break out in a sweat and have to dive out. It took me a long time to be able to even talk to a woman, and that's why you needn't have any fear of me.'

What sounded like a big sigh came from the bed.

'So you haven't been with a woman for ten years?' Sarah asked. Tom shook his head. 'You mean you've never had sexual relief in all that time?' she asked incredulously.

'Oh yes,' Tom replied. 'I can do it to myself, looking at pictures and…and…other things.' He'd nearly said by looking through windows at others.

'You poor man,' Sarah said softly. 'So that was the last time that you've touched a woman or had one touch you?'

'That was the last time,' he simply said. She half sat up in the bed, the covers grasped up over her breasts.

'Tom,' she said his name slowly, stretching it out softly into two syllables. 'Tom, come here. Next to me.' Tom rose from the chair and stood by the bed. 'Sit down,' she said quietly. He sat down most gingerly on the edge of the bed. 'Touch my face. Gently. Just brush your fingers against my cheek.' Tom slowly put out his hand and it jumped back to his side as the tips of his fingers touched her lightly. 'Again, Tom.' He extended his arm again and touched her face, but still withdrew his hand immediately. She pulled her arm out from the covers. He flinched and started to rise, but she said, 'No, Tom. Stay there. I won't touch you.' She laid her arm alongside her body. He could see her tanned shoulder gleaming as it caught the soft light.

'Now touch my arm,' she said softly, 'and hold it.' Tom touched her arm and held it. He gripped it rather hard and she winced. 'Gently, Tom, gently and relax. Just let yourself relax. Let me help you.' He relaxed and held her arm lightly. 'Now run your hand up and down my arm. See. You can do it. Put your hand up higher, to my shoulder.' His hand moved up and he rested it on her bare shoulder. Her other hand came slowly out from under the bed clothes and covered his hand. He started to move away but she then held his hand tight. 'I said relax, Tom. Let my hand move for you. Let's work together to help you.' She gently slid his hand off her shoulder and underneath the covers. He felt his hand slide down and onto the firm swelling of the top of her breast. His hand stopped there, held by the pressure of hers.

'Relax, Tom. I don't mind, really I don't. Let me help,' and she forced his hand down till it covered the nipple of her breast. He could feel the soft bump under his palm and felt it start to stiffen as she moved his hand back and forth across it. His fingers could feel the swell of her breast as it rounded down to her lower chest. 'Now do it yourself, Tom,' she whispered. 'I'll take my hand away and you do it yourself.' He felt her hand leave his and he managed to keep his hand moving. He forced a grin to his face and gave out a shaky laugh.

Slowly over the next hour, she took his hand on a private conducted tour of her body. She had drawn the covers right off and he was able to gaze at her naked body without wanting to run away. Looking at a woman's body through a disguised mirror and seeing one within touching distance were totally different realities for Tom. He felt a great surge of triumph at being able to do this. He was running his hand over a naked woman's body and he felt great, but it was not having the desired effect that it would have to a normal male. Sarah could see this and decided on a gamble.

'Tom,' and again his name was a drawn out call. 'Go into the bathroom and get undressed. When you come back in here I'll be right under the covers. You won't see me and I won't see you. Then you slide into this bed. But don't touch me.' He had started to protest but at her last words, kept silent and went off to the bathroom and stripped right down. He looked at himself in the mirror for it wasn't a body to be ashamed of. His stomach was flat and solid and not any excess fat anywhere. The only problem of fat he thought sadly, was the piece between his legs that hung there quite limp. He went back into the bedroom quite fearfully and was relieved to see that she had done as she said she would. He could make out her shape lying on the edge of the far side of the bed. He gingerly lifted the covers and slid in and lay there rigid, holding his breath.

'Tom?' his name was asked from under the covers. 'Put your hand out and touch me,' Sarah's muffled voice said. He did this several times, the contact being very brief and within a few minutes, she was so close to him that he could feel her body heat though they were not actually touching.

'Why don't you pull down the covers so that you can see me and I can see you?' It took him quite some time for him to be able to do this but he could really see that wonderful body that he had viewed from the office window. 'I'm tired now, Tom,' she said sleepily. 'You don't mind if I go off to sleep. Leave the covers off for it's so warm in here.' He nodded and didn't flinch this time as her hand came in contact with his chest as she settled on her side facing him. Her eyes were closed and Tom turned his head and saw her face composed for sleep. He liked the beauty of it lying so close to him.

His gaze went down to her lovely breasts there, a scant six inches away from him. Her flat stomach that sloped down to the pubic hairs of her sex, her tanned thighs turning into shapely legs with perfect ankles.

Her hand still lay on his chest and it moved slightly as she settled herself in a half sleep. She gave several sighs and each time, her hand moved and it seemed to move of its own accord. Sometimes the fingers would twitch and then the hand would move in a slow caressing motion. Tom watched in fascination as it slowly moved down his chest, across his stomach and came to rest at the edge of his pubic hairs. He tentatively raised his arm so that his hand came up and he gently brushed her breast with it. As she didn't move, he grew bolder and turned his body slightly so that his hand could cup the breast it was touching. As he did so, her hand fell down to his crotch and was laying against his limp prick. He kept still and held his breath for a moment before he slowly moved himself over so that he could bend his head and touched his lips to her nipple.

His head shot back as she stirred and her hand flexed and grasped his prick, not tightly, but with a firm coolness. He bent his head again and took the nipple ever so gently into his mouth and began to suck on it. He was as pleased as punch in doing this, knowing he'd overcome a major stumbling block in his sex life. He felt her hand move and his prick flop about lightly in her grasp. She moved slightly and he saw that her eyes were open for she hadn't been sleeping.

'Lay back, Tom,' she said softly, 'and let me help.' He lay back as she rose up and moved herself further down the bed. He could see the contrast between her tanned body and his pale white colour and made a mental note to try and get some sunbathing in next year. He felt her hair trail across his stomach and it raised goose bumps on his arms. He also felt her lips kiss him firmly on the insides of his thighs and brush across his flaccid tool as well. As he hadn't flinched, she took the plunge and took his cock firmly into her mouth. He felt her hot flesh clamp on him and he lay there with mixed emotions.

At that moment he felt love for Sarah. For her youth, her sun tanned body and what she was doing for him. With this new feeling he could also feel a surge of power and it came as a shock that he felt this power now manifesting itself through his cock. Her hot mouth and tongue were helping to increase the size and she soon had to release him to catch her breath. She renewed her attack with vigour and he could feel heat rising in his balls. She came back up the bed gasping for air and lay back next to him.

'It's there, Tom,' she whispered excitedly. 'You've done it! Look at it. You've got it beat. Now try it, Tom, please, with me. Try it.' Her earlier experience of the evening was dead in her mind. She felt excitement at what she had achieved. Tom timidly rolled over and got onto his knees and knelt between her open thighs. She smiled at him encouragingly.

'Now, Tom,' she whispered. 'Put it where it belongs.' She held the lips of her sex open and guided him into her warm softness. Tom let himself slide down till he was firmly embedded in her and lying full length on top of her. He could feel her firm tits below his chest, and his own breast swelled with pride as he started to fuck her. And fuck he did. He was like a young colt feeling his oats for the first time. He pumped himself dry into her and she was delighted as she climaxed herself. Tom was a contented man when he dropped off to sleep with his face pressed into Sarah's breasts. She too drifted off to sleep, her hand firmly holding Tom's new lease of life prick.

TOM WOKE up late, later than usual. He would have slept longer but he was experiencing the pleasant sensation that aroused him and he could see Sarah's head between his legs, tonguing his prick into an instant erection. Her face was aglow with joy when she lifted her head and saw he was awake. She rose up and straddled him and holding his erection upright, lowered herself down onto it.

He watched his cock disappear inside her and marvelled again at the sight of her perfectly tanned body, now clearly visible in the daylight and loved what she was doing as she worked herself up and down on his tool. Her hands cupped those lovely twin mounds with the nipples standing out and her face with its rapturous smile warmed Tom's heart as he felt the heat from his balls start to surge up. He started to move himself, humping his hips upwards to her grinding down on him. She threw her head back and began to give out a gurgling cry and Tom cried out too as they came together at the same time. His seed was sent upwards to mix and mingle with her juices that came down. She fell forward over him and he loved the feel of her tightness, gripping his prick firmly and her tits pressing his chest, her warm breath on his neck and the sweet smell of her hair that had fallen across his face.

'Sarah, Sarah,' he whispered into her hair, 'dear Sarah,' and held her close to him. She too loved the taut feeling of the insides of her body as she held him tight within her. She also felt so secure with his surprisingly strong arms holding her firmly as she rocked herself in his embrace. He in turn was stroking her naked back and as she raised her head and face up to him, he kissed her gently on the lips.

'Thank you, Sarah. Thank you very much.' She smiled at him, her eyes really alight. 'But I've still got a motel to run,' he said, trying to disengage himself from her. She gave out a small whimper as his prick slipped out of her warm body and rolled off of him. Her tits bounced excitedly as she jumped off the bed.

'Bags the bathroom first,' she said with a smile and he grinned as her pert bum jiggled out of the room and into the bathroom.

They had showered and were dressing when Tom suddenly felt himself deflate emotionally for she would now be leaving, he thought. She was thinking that now he'll throw me out, wham, bam thank you ma-am, goodbye. Both were very silent as they finished dressing and when done, moved about the room as if in a trance, both having troubled thoughts.

'Tom.'

'Sarah,' they both had started to speak at the same time and laughed a little self-consciously and Tom looked at his watch.

'Sarah?' he said, looking again at his watch. 'Today is Sunday and it's time now that I usually go to church. Would you like to come with me?'

Her heart gave a leap.

'Yes, Tom,' she breathed out fast. 'I'd love to.' He looked at her and grinned.

'Come on then,' and held out his hand to her. They went first to her hostel where within a few minutes, she was able to change into something more suitable for church going.

The Reverend Tyler was at the church door greeting those entering the church for worship. Tom and Sarah got a seat in a pew near the front and sat and held hands till the service started. Tom could see in the front pew on the other aisle, the Reverend's wife and children. Madelene, the eldest daughter was on the end and he could see her well-shaped breast outlined under the calico dress as it tightened when she half turned to see who was in the church. He remembered the time he had seen that breast, and the other of the pair, in the flesh. Not only her tits but her pussy as well.

It was not long after he'd opened the motel and not all the cabins had been let. A couple of the town's lads had wanted to book a cabin and so Tom let them. When he viewed the room later he found that there were four boys and two girls in the cabin. A record player was going full blast though nobody seemed to be paying any attention to it. They were all laying about the room in various stages of undress and all smoking. He knew straight away that they were smoking pot. This he didn't like. If he was raided, he would be in one hell of a spot even though they were all over eighteen years old. Well one of the girls was this Madelene Tyler, the Reverend's daughter, though she preferred to be called Madge. She was wearing just a bra and panties and laying on the bed. A boy by the name of Jim, son of the garage owner, was lying down beside her. He was only wearing a pair of faded blue jeans.

Also in the cabin was Fred Dale, the druggist's son and Willy Smith whose father worked for the railroad. The other boy Tom didn't know. The other girl with them was Penny Lane who lived with her aunt on Orchard Street. She was wearing the same as Madge but a filmy bra and matching panties. Fred Dale was down to his pants and was gently stroking Penny's thigh. The other two boys were still dressed, except for shoes, the standard dress for youngsters those days, faded jeans and sweat shirts. The air of the cabin was hazy with smoke from the cigarettes they were smoking

Jim, on the bed with Madge, finished his cigarette and rolled to her and slipped a bra strap off and uncovered one of her small tits. He then took it into his mouth and lay there sucking on it. She carried on smoking completely oblivious of what was going on down at her exposed breast. Penny had her hand into the pants of Fred and had just pulled his cock free and was slowly rubbing it up and down.

The boy Tom didn't know, stood up and shucked off his jeans and shorts and stood in front of Penny with his prick standing out in front of him. She stubbed out her cigarette and took it in her hand and pulled him closer to her and took his cock into her mouth and started giving him a blow job on him while still giving Fred his hand job. Willy Smith watched the two for a moment before he too stood up and stripped off. He went over to the bed and pulled down Madge's panties from her legs and dropped them on the floor. He opened her legs, which didn't show any resistance and buried his head between her thighs and proceeded to lick her out.

This brought some reaction for she dropped her cigarette somewhere and tried to unzip Jim's fly. But with him sucking her tit, she couldn't reach it. She angrily pushed his head off her and sat up. Her bare tit was all red round the nipple where he had been sucking the blood to the under surface of the skin. Willy's head still kept bobbing between her legs though it was more difficult now for him with her sitting up. She shrugged off her bra so that both tits were now free. She grabbed Jim's fly and deftly pulled out his erection and started to pump it in her hand.

Not a word had been spoken by any of them, mind you, if they had uttered any words, no one would have heard them above the noise of the record player. Willy raised his head, his eyes unfocused and his lips and chin smeared from the juices of Madge. He struggled to his knees, his thin cock bouncing lightly. Madge shook her head and pushed Jim down the bed and beckoned to Willy. Jim managed to get down to the end of the bed, almost falling off before getting in between her legs and sticking his cock up into her and begin to fuck her. Madge helped Willy get his leg astride the top of her body. Jim's head kept hitting him in the back, knocking him forward so Willy shifted further up till his head was resting on the mirror and his cock just above the mouth of Madge.

Tom had to shift his position in the locker to be able to see them properly. With Jim ramming himself into her, she lifted her head and took Willy's cock into her mouth and used her head as a pump as she mouthed his erection as best as she could in that awkward position. The smoking of the pot must have slowed them all down because it took them some time to reach their peaks.

Willy came first. With him bucking his cock in her mouth, it came out just as he started to come, sending his sperm up all over her face. She partly turned her head and shut her eyes, her mouth gaping frantically as she tried to recapture that red pumping piece of flesh with its surge of semen jetting out. His contents smeared her cheek and glued her eyes shut and went into her hair too. Then Jim came, pulling himself out of her wet cunt and let his load jerk in spasms out across her stomach and drip into her pubic hairs.

He laughed at this and wiped the end of his cock on the side of her thigh before helping Willy climb off of her. The other boy on seeing what had happened there, pulled his cock out of Penny's mouth and went over to the bed and grabbed Madge's arm and lifted it up. He then put his large cock under her armpit and brought her arm down again, trapping his cock there. He then started to fuck her armpit as the other boys laughed. She was using her free hand to try and clear the sticky semen from her eyes when Fred, who had left Penny too, came to the other side of the bed and finished off the hand job that Penny had been giving him.

He started to come, his hand moving faster and then guided his streaming sperm to cover her tits. She tried to push him away and free her other arm and twisted her head just as the other boy began to come. It caught her square on the nose and then pumped out onto her neck and chin. Penny had come over to the side of the bed and the boys grabbed her and pulled off her bra and panties and pushed her so that she fell on top of Madge. They pulled and pushed her so that she was flat on top and then moved her about so that she too got smeared with their semen. Penny laughed in delight and started kissing Madge and licking her face. Madge's arms went round Penny and the two girls squirmed about on the bed really covering themselves in the mess.

Sarah nudged Tom and brought his mind back to where he was. They sung the hymns and then sat back down to listen to the sermon. It was Sodom and Gomorrah again and Tom groaned inwardly for he knew what that meant. He looked at the choir boys sitting in their pews and wondered which one it would be today, though he would find out during the afternoon.

His mind went back to the Reverend's daughter and Penny Lane thrashing about on the bed. They had completely smothered themselves in the boys' juices and then proceeded to clean each other with their mouths and tongues. It took quite some time. The boys enjoyed the spectacle and so had Tom. All the more when he met her on Sundays and knew exactly what she looked like under the stiff formal Sunday clothes and just what she was capable of doing. He would never let the boys have a cabin again for he didn't like the idea of them smoking pot because that could cause him more trouble than the sex side of things.

With the sermon finished and a last prayer, Tom and Sarah left the church and went out into the bright sunshine. He felt ten foot tall walking down the road holding the hand of this tall beautiful well built, sun tanned walking dream. Just the fact of being able to hold the hand of a member of the opposite sex out in public was a major achievement for him and just that very morning he had actually fucked her. Fucked the first woman since Caroline those many years ago.

He asked her if she would have lunch with him and she said she would be delighted to and so they stopped off at the diner. When they'd finished, he said that he had to check to see that all the cabins had been cleaned properly and would she like to watch television in his cabin until he'd finished. She said she would and so they went back to the motel and he got the television out of the office and set it up in his room.

He cleaned the office first before checking the cabins and making sure that number seven was in good condition and had just finished when the Reverend Tyler arrived. Every Sunday after lunch, he came to the motel having booked number seven for his afternoon meditation as he called it. The glass walls of this cabin helped him to see himself as the Lord saw him. Dirty bastard, thought Tom. The Lord sees and so do I, he said to himself. The choir boy carrying the Reverend's books was Billy Walker. You wouldn't have guessed to look at this perfect little angel that he was eighteen though he looked as if he was only twelve, the dirty little fucker.

When the Reverend's sermon was about Sodom and Gomorrah, Tom knew that it would definitely be one of the choirboys. If it was about Jezebel, the painted harlot, then it would be one of the young women of the Sunday league who would come to meditate with him. With the other sermons, it would be pot luck who he brought with him.

He gave over the key and finished off the cleaning of the office before going along to the locker for cabin number seven to see what chapter they were up to. Both were naked and young Billy was bent over the chair, holding the sides with his hands, his little prick standing out from his sparse bush. The Right Reverend Tyler was into his meditation with Billy, for he was well and truly stuck up the boy's arse. His bony prick was going in and out of the boy's tight arsehole like a piston engine. He was standing behind him holding onto the narrow hips and pumping his own arse backwards and forwards, his prick sliding in and out. The boy was obviously getting as much pleasure out of it as Tyler was. All the time he was stuffing the boy, he was looking into the different mirrors watching himself doing it from all angles. His mouth was slack and a little spittle ran down his chin as he saw himself a dozen times lunging into the arsehole between the little white cheeks of the boy's bum with every stroke. Tyler shuddered and his thin shanks quivered as he came inside the boy, holding the hips tight up to his thighs as he jerked.

After coming, he pulled his cock out of the tight little hole and went through to the bathroom to wash himself for he never used a condom. The boy knew the routine for he went and got onto the bed and laid on his back, his small cock hard and tight and lying up on his lower stomach. Tyler came back in and got on the bed laying in the opposite direction and immediately began to suck on the boy's cock. He was able to take the whole thing into his mouth and also played with the balls in their sac below. By turning his head as he sucked he could again see many pictures of himself in this act and also of the boy who was now sucking on the Reverend's limp washed cock.

Tom jerked the curtains back across the window and stomped out of the locker. The sonofabitch, he said to himself as he went back over to his cabin. The dirty sonofabitch, I should kick him straight out on his ass. But then the Reverend would put out the word against him. He could tell Billy Walker's parents, but no. That was no good for he looked to be enjoying it and who would believe his word against the Reverend and Billy? He kicked his cabin door open and went inside.

He'd forgot Sarah was in there. He started with surprise as she rushed over to him. Startled, he fell back against the door jamb. Sarah suddenly stopped on seeing his face.

'Oh, sorry Tom. I forgot. I've just been watching a lovely film and felt so happy, then you came in so I jumped up to kiss you.' She dropped her voice a little. 'Can I kiss you, Tom?' He laughed having recovered himself and held out his arms.

'Of course you can. I forgot you were here and you startled me.' She went into his arms slowly and gave him a quick kiss and pulled herself away to look at him.

'You touched and kissed me without any problems. I'm glad that we talked last night.'

'Sarah,' Tom said hesitantly, 'I…I…don't know really how to thank you for what you've done for me. You…you've managed to change my life so much in just one night. I…I…' he broke off and wandered about the room, touching small things to avoid looking at her. 'You have the most perfect figure I've ever seen, and… and…I am most humbly touched that you helped me with it last night. I…I…well Sarah, I would like it if you could stay again tonight as well.' He stood with his back to her when he finished speaking, and stood there waiting for her to answer him.

He heard her move across the room and felt her arms go over his shoulders and saw her hands locking front of him. Her breasts were pushing into his back and her stomach and thighs were pressed tight up against him. She lay her head on his shoulder, her face turned towards his.

'Tom, I would love to stay the night. Tonight. Tomorrow night, and the night after. I will stay as long as you want me to, if you'll let me.' She spoke the last very softly. He turned without breaking her hold of him and held her tight to him. Pressing her close and feeling the warmth of her body through their clothes.

He felt himself starting to rise up, a wonderful feeling that he hadn't been able to do for years without watching somebody else having sex. To touch a woman in the flesh and feel his pecker rise to the occasion. She felt him getting hard too and grinned at him.

'The therapy worked,' she whispered. He broke the contact between them before he could speak, and then it was only in a strangled voice.

'Let me see to the motel first, then we can spend all night here. I'll only be in the office next door seeing to the guests coming in. When they are all in, then, then....'

'Can I come and sit in the office with you? I want to be with you all the time,' she said. He took her hand and gave it a squeeze and led her out of the cabin and into the office.

Some of the guests were early and they booked in and were given their keys and the Reverend Tyler checked out, giving Tom his key, thanking him very much. Tom watched him go saying to himself that he would one day give him what he deserved. He told Sarah that there were a couple of cabins keys still to be collected. Would she see that the people signed in when they came while he saw to cabin seven and got it ready for occupancy. She said that she understood and he left her in charge of the office.

With cabin seven that the Reverend had just vacated, it was only a matter of straightening the bed covers and changing the used towels for clean ones to make it ready for the next guest. He saw somebody checking in and that Sarah seemed to be coping and so he thought he'd have a quick look round to see if all was okay in the other cabins. He was passing cabin three and decided to look in and see what they were doing. He unlocked the door to the locker and went inside and drew the curtain aside. It was early in the evening but the occupants were already stripped off for action.

It was big Fred again with the same red haired girl that he was with in cabin six, the water bed. They were in the sixty nine position and really basting themselves. Fred digging his tongue into her wet sex while she was really pulling his large prick into her mouth as she sucked on him. Last time, the girl had been unprepared for the lift up that he gave her so that his cock was rammed right into her throat but she was ready for it this time.

He lifted her up in one movement and held her above his swollen cock and she grasped it with her hand and took the head of it into her mouth and relaxed as he lowered her down onto it. Tom watched fascinated as he saw the hard outline of it pass direct into her gullet. So engrossed in the scene, Tom did not hear the door of the locker open and close. Nor the sound of somebody step up close and stop just behind him. He heard the gasp though and whirled round and there stood Sarah. In all the times he'd visited the lockers, this was the first time that he had forgotten to lock the door behind him.

'She'll choke,' she gasped, her hand up to her own throat as if to massage it.

'What the hell are you doing in here,' Tom managed to get out in his anger at seeing her there. 'You should be in the office.' She stood looking through the viewing with her eyes wide. Spoke falteringly but without taking her eyes off the scene of big Fred pumping the red haired girl up and down on his prick.

'I…I saw you come in here and I came to…to tell you that…that all the guests had…had arrived…and…and that we could, how can…it's not possible. She'll choke to death like that!' Tom tried to move her, but she was rooted to the spot watching.

'Out,' said Tom. 'Come on, out!'

'No. Wait a minute. Please Tom, just a minute. Let me see what happens.' She was still wide eyed watching and Tom looked and saw the finale as big Fred shot his load. You could see the shape of his cock throb and spasm as his seed jetted up deep into her throat. He then lifted her right off, his arm muscles tightly knotted and covered in a thin film of sweat as he did so and plunked her down on the bed.

'That was better than last time eh?' Fred chuckled. The red head grinned at him as she rubbed her throat.

'You're still a big fucking bastard,' she said and ducked and laughed as his hand flew at her head and missed. She threw herself on top of him and wrestled him as she grunted out, 'Now let's put that big fucking tool that you've got where it rightly belongs. It's my turn now.' Fred gave his chuckling laugh and rolled her over. Tom pulled the curtain across the window and turned angrily to Sarah.

'Well?' he demanded. 'You've seen it now.' She clutched at his arm.

'Tom, quick,' she said excitedly. 'Let's go to your cabin. That has got me so worked up.' She pulled at his arm and he followed her out with an air of puzzled wonderment. He had expected all sorts of foul oaths and such like to be heaped upon him by Sarah for doing such a thing as watching other people having sex. But she had got excited by the sight and wanted nothing more than to work it off with Tom. He managed to free his arm from her grasp and lock the locker behind him. She feverishly grabbed his arm again and hurried him along to his cabin. Inside, she turned and held him tight as she rubbed herself up against him.

'Tom, Tom, let's get into bed. Seeing them has made me want you, quick. Earlier I had wanted to go slow and play at seducing you, but I can't wait now.' She was pulling at his shirt, one button coming away completely. He finished taking his shirt off and then his trousers while she quickly stripped off her dress and underthings and spread herself on her back on the bed. Tom still had his shorts and socks to get off and then stood by the bed, his own prick was, to his delight, standing out ready for combat.

'No playing about, Tom,' she begged. 'I'm ready now. Please, darling.' Tom still had to wait a moment just to look at the body stretched out for him. Her big round breasts, the flat stomach, the fine legs wide open so that he could see her snatch waiting for him. It was wet and juicy and ready to lubricate his prick on its entry. 'Please, Tom! Come and make love to me.' He climbed on the bed between her legs and dipped his wick into the holder.

He slid in with ease as her legs swung up so that his whole length could enter. He dug deep and worked his hips from side to side as he pumped in and out. She bucked her hips in time with him and exploded in a burst of juices which he felt spurt down alongside his prick and smear the tops of his thighs. He kept working his meat inside her, feeling the wet sides of her vagina trying to grip his shaft tight. He felt the pressure building up in his balls and increased his pace until his sperm erupted out of his cock inside her. She held him tight as he lay on top of her, crooning softly in his ear. They lay for a little while like this until he began to withdraw but she held him even tighter.

'No!' She whispered fiercely. 'Stay there awhile. Let me keep it inside of me for it's so nice and fulfilling. Keep it in there.' He lay still on top of her as he gently stroked her hair and kissing her eyelids, nose and lips in gentle little bird pecks. He could feel her working the muscles inside her vagina, pressing his prick in different places at the same time and it started to respond and expand.

'My darling,' she whispered. 'It's getting bigger again. Come, now. Do it slowly this time. I want to feel your hardness in me. Fuck me gently, Tom.' Tom slowly began to move himself backwards and forwards inside and so gently fucked her.

They lay side by side, nestled together. His body pale and white which had not seen the sun for many years, contrasting sharply with her golden tanned flesh. His hand gently caressed the breast that hung towards him and he playfully tweaked the hard nipple. She moved slightly from this and opened her eyes.

'Tom,' she drawled out his name slowly and softly. 'Looking into the room, is that the way, the only way you could have sex?' He turned his head to hers on the pillow and kissed her nose.

'Yes. I could get it up by looking at other people having fun, but I couldn't if face to face with a woman.'

'How terrible for you,' she said. 'Having to watch other people having their sex while you couldn't do it the same way.' He didn't say that he got extreme pleasure from watching other people. 'I bet you saw some strange sights.' Tom chuckled.

'You bet! You'd be surprised at the number of men who come here with somebody else's wife or girlfriend, and some girls who come with other girls.' He chuckled again. 'I think that nearly all the top people of this town have spent one night here. There would be some very red faces about this burg if they knew all that I know. They'd pay a fortune to keep me quiet.' He lay there shaking with silent laughter. Sarah propped herself up on an elbow and drew a fingernail up and down his chest.

'Tom, have you ever thought of making any money out of that fact?'

'What fact?' he asked.

'Well, you just said that the people of this town would pay a small fortune if you didn't say who was with who here.'

'So they would, the sanctimonious bastards. Like the Right fucking Reverend Tyler for one. Buggering a choirboy every Sunday afternoon. I'd like to knock that pious look off his face. But who'd believe my word against his?'

'What if you had some photos? Then it wouldn't matter what he said, would it now? You'd have proof.'

'Yeah, well, that would be blackmail, wouldn't it?'

'Well, in a way it would. But not if you did it to show up the hypocrites. That would change their tune. If you didn't ask for money or anything, then it isn't blackmail.'

'Whichever way you put it, it's still blackmail,' he said.

'Tom. Look at me.' He turned his head and looked at her. He could spend the rest of his life just looking at her sweet face, he thought.

'Tom. I don't mean to be rude or personal. I'm not asking for myself but I'm thinking of you, well, I would also like to think....well I...I...mean...I like you, Tom. I would like to stay with you, if...if...you would have me stay.' She had dropped her eyes, but still kept her finger moving on his chest. He reached for her but she pushed his hand back. 'No, wait a minute, I haven't finished. What I was trying to say was, how much money do you have in the bank? I don't mean how much, but I'm thinking that if they found out about your windows? I mean, what would happen to you then?' Tom chuckled.

'I think they would sling me in jail for a few weeks and close the place down.'

'That's what I mean,' she stressed. 'Do you have enough to get another place if by mischance they found out and this happened?' Tom stopped chuckling and lost himself in thought and slowly shook his head.

'No. I wouldn't have enough to open another place. You're not thinking of blackmailing me, are you?' She flung herself on top of him and tears came to her eyes and began to run down her face and fell onto his below hers.

'No, Tom. I couldn't do that to you. Don't you realize, you big fool, I've fallen in love with you and I wouldn't want to see you hurt.' She dropped her head onto his shoulder sobbing. He stroked the back of her head and could feel her heaving chest pressing those fine full orbs into him. These and the warmth of her thigh brought his cock up into the night air and he swallowed a lump in his throat that this young girl loved him. She felt his prick rise against the side of her thigh and she choked back a sob with a short laugh and grasped it firmly in her fist.

'Well, this loves me.' Tom then pushed her back and mounted her and slid his prick into her inner warmth.

'I love you too, Sarah. I really do love you.' He covered her face with kisses as he slowly moved his hips back and forth.

'Well, really love me then,' she purred back at him and locked her legs over his hips. 'Love me again and again and again.' They moved in unison and Tom surged forward, diving his cock deep into the neck of her womb and sending his love into her in savage bursts from the fiery end.

Sated, they lay as before, nestled together and gently stroked each other in silence for a while.

'Tom,' Sarah spoke, breaking that silence. 'It wouldn't cost a lot of money to buy a movie camera and the equipment to get it all set up. Then as long as you get enough on film so that if anything did happen, you'd be alright then, do you see?' He did see alright, but since they had laid down, he had given it some serious thought. Yes he had enough money to buy the equipment, he still had quite a bit left from the bank robber's haul stashed away. But it was the ethics of it that troubled him.

Not only that, because once he started blackmailing people, they would never ever come back to the motel again and in time, would tell other people not to use it. They would say that they'd heard rumours about the place. Word would get round and he'd lose any further sources of money from the town if he took this route.

Yet again, if someone might decide that instead of paying for the film, hire a hit man to either wipe or burn him out. This was a powerful reason as to why he should say no to this idea before it even got off the ground.

They argued for an hour and she eventually had to agree with him that it would in the long term destroy the motel, but countered that they could still do the filming as insurance. If anyone that they had on film wanted for whatever reason, to try and cause any trouble for him, he would then have a counter argument. So it was agreed that they would do the filming but not to be used for blackmailing purposes but purely as an insurance policy.

'Oh Tom, I do love you. I really feel that I do,' Sarah said as she hugged and kissed him. 'So much so that I want you to do to me what we saw in that cabin.'

'Not bloody likely!' he said. 'I'm not as strong as Fred.'

'Well, what if we tried it a different way?' Tom's prick started to rise at this thought. 'See! He thinks it would be nice,' she exclaimed as she took hold of it and gave it a rub. She bounced up on the bed and dragged Tom up. 'Get off the bed a minute.' He did as he was asked and got off and stood by the side with his erection standing upright in front of him as she sorted herself out and lay across the bed to hang her head right over the edge where he was standing so that she was looking at him upside down. Her hair was trailing on the floor and she tried to speak but found she couldn't in that position and had to lift her head up. 'Like this, Tom.'

She let her head drop back again and lifted her arms and grabbed his hands and pulled him down so that he was on his knees facing her, his prick waving about just in front of her nose. She lifted her head up again and half turned towards him.

'I think we can manage it. Be gentle though. I will try to relax myself as much as possible, but if I slap you hard, pull out for it will be hurting me.' She rolled back so that her head hung over the edge of the bed again. Tom leaned forward and placed his hands on the bed and let her take his cock into her hand and guide it into her mouth. He saw and felt the head of his prick slide in between her teeth and enter her throat. He felt her gag and started to pull back but she held him by her hands behind the cheeks of his bum. He was amazed to feel his erection slide right in so that his balls touched her nose. He slowly bent forward until he could reach those lovely breasts just below him and gently gave them a squeeze before moving up straight.

Her hands started to move his arse so his cock moved in and out of her mouth and throat and the sensation he was getting through his prick was fantastic. Tighter than her cunt could ever have been. Her saliva had lubricated his cock so that it was able to move and he very slowly and gently began to fuck her deep inside her throat, marvelling at the fact that he could see himself moving inside.

He had to hold himself rigid as he felt his semen come surging up his prick and belching out of the end directly into her stomach. When it finished its own pumping, he slowly withdrew it from her throat. Back into her mouth and back past her teeth. It was a wonderful and powerful feeling to be able to do this to a girl. She rolled over when he was free and rubbed her throat.

'That hurt,' she croaked out. She held out her arms and he got up and rolled onto the bed with her. 'We won't be doing that for a long time; besides, I don't get the pleasure you get. I'd rather just take the head into my mouth to suck and tease it with my tongue, and that's how much I love you, Tom. I love you so much that I would do anything for you. Anything!' He held her tight as he savoured the word, anything. They finally and sleepily kissed each other good night till they fell asleep with their arms tightly wound about each other.

They awoke early next morning, Tom with a steaming hard on which Sarah was delighted with and was soon astride him, taking him inside herself. He loved to see her up on top with her breasts bouncing lovely in time to her movements that he could fondle, the coupling culminating in him coming with some force inside her. Though she hated the withdrawal of his cock, she was quickly off of him to suck on his still erect, steaming cock to pull out what juices he still had left in the hard shaft that would soon wilt. With both of them satisfied, they had their shower and got dressed and she then acted as a wife and prepared them breakfast in the kitchen in the office while Tom saw to the departing guests.

After eating, at her request, Tom took her into cabins one to seven to see what delights they held for certain of the guests who stayed there. She shuddered in cabin one thinking of the story Tom had told her of his army experience, being strung up and beaten. The same for cabin two on seeing the rack with him explaining that she'd be surprised at the number of sadists and masochists that were around. She liked the leather touch of cabin three and when she saw cabin four with all the phallic brass hooks and posts, wanted to try it out some time. She cooed with delight at both cabins five and six, rolling on the fur covered bed and bouncing on the water one. In cabin seven she even took her top off so that she could see her breasts seven times over from the angled mirrors and this delighted Tom too. They didn't bother with the other three cabins for they were same as Tom's.

She marvelled at the mirrors he had installed saying that you couldn't tell from inside the cabins that you could be viewed from the other side.

As Tom didn't expect any guests to arrive till late afternoon, He ran Sarah into town to the hostel where she had been staying for her to collect her things. Next stop was the photographer's shop where she had been working and told them that she wouldn't be going there anymore. The owner didn't like her leaving without proper notice but there was nothing he could do about it.

They went back to the motel where she fixed a light lunch for them and then sat in the office with him to discuss what they should buy in the city the next day. He also showed her the motel's books which were easy to keep and found that it didn't take much learning to know how to run the office. It was also agreed that they would give it a few days before giving Mrs Towser her notice and for Sarah to help Tom in the cleaning of the motel, giving the woman a month's wages in lieu of the proper notice.

After dinner with the motel full, he didn't go and do any viewing for he now had Sarah to look at and loved the striptease she did for him as she slowly revealed her luscious body to his gaze. The difference now being the fact that he could handle what he saw and soon had an erection which she was delighted to see and have him join her in bed and be fucked by him.

After breakfast and another performance of sex between them, they went off to the city in his pick-up. They had already discussed what equipment they would need for the filming and processing, the latter she would do having learned this at the shop where she had worked. They would use the kitchen as their dark room for this purpose. Tom took enough money and they visited several shops to select all that they would need. A sixteen mm movie camera and fast film for any dim lighting in the cabin. The proper lights for the dark room as well as the developing trays and chemicals to be used and also more infra-red bulbs for the cabins. They also bought a projector and screen and an enlarger for any still prints that they might make.

They were away four hours and Mrs Towser was pleased with the little cash bonus for minding the office while they had been out. After a quick lunch, they went and set up the camera on a tripod in the locker for cabin eight as this would be the one selected for this coming night's filming.

She did some test filming of Tom in the cabin with his changing of the lights to see how the film would come out. She had to laugh at his antics in front of the mirror as she made her adjustments and even got him on film with his penis out of his trousers as he waggled it about while standing on the bed and even got to press it up against the mirror while she was running the test film through.

Tom watched as Sarah fitted out the kitchen as her dark room. Laying out the trays and chemicals, fixing up a drying line, changing the bulbs and having him help her put up a heavy curtain across the doorway.

She processed this clip and was satisfied that all was working well and that the lighting was good enough even having had the cabin in complete darkness but with the unseen infra-red light on. So all was ready for the occupants of this cabin this coming evening. That would be, to Tom's delight, Judge Walter Hopkins, the town's local presiding judge. He had a guess who would be his companion for the evening and he was right when he saw that it was Constance Mason. She was the wife of a young barrister who went off on a circuit once every three months.

When the judge gave him good verdicts in his client's favour as they came before him, Mason thought it was because of his eloquence in the court room. He did not know that his wife secured these verdicts in Tom's motel.

It was quite dark as it always was when the judge entered the office to collect his key, so that he would not be seen and possibly be recognised by other guests. Tom nervously gave him his key as the judge put a false name in the register. All irregular but the judge had promised Tom a large hamper at Christmas. He took his key and Tom watched him go down and help a female out of his car and they quickly disappeared in the direction of cabin eight.

Tom went to his cabin and told Sarah that they had arrived and that they should go there straight away for the judge usually only stayed for a couple of hours as he had a wife at home. They quickly went down to the locker for number eight and going inside and carefully locking the door behind them. Tom drew back the curtain and light from the room flooded the locker. Sarah shrank back from the window with a gasp as Tom held her and explained that the cabin's occupants could neither see nor hear them, but they, in the locker, could see and hear all that went on in their room.

Tom was correct in his assumption as to who the judge's partner would be. Constance Mason was seated at the dressing table taking her earrings off. The judge had been in the bathroom and now came into the room as Constance took off her blouse, draped it over the chair and started to brush her hair. It was a luxurious auburn colour that fell in natural waves down to her shoulders. The judge, just into his fifties had an abundant shock of white hair which contrasted sharply with his thick black bushy eyebrows. He was unbuttoning his shirt as he crossed the room and bent and kissed the back of her neck. She didn't pause in the brushing of her hair as he did so.

'Come on, Connie. Cut out the cold shoulder act,' he said exasperatedly, but she continued brushing her hair for a few more strokes before slamming down the brush to swing round to face him. Her eyes flashed fire, giving her otherwise plain features a spark of life, unlike her normal shop window mannequin expression.

'Well? Does Phillip get a nomination or not for the D.A.'s job?' Phillip being her husband. 'For the last three months you've been saying that you'll think about it. Well it's now gone on long enough. Does he get the nomination or not?'

'Now, Connie…'

'Don't you now Connie me!' she interrupted. Just a straight answer or I'll start saying that I'll think about it. Whether I stay here now or go home,' she paused for breath and effect, 'or drop a few hints about us in high places,' she threatened and whirled round to face the mirror again and started to re-brush her hair.

'Now, Conn…Constance. Don't talk like that,' he said as he moved in closer and put his hands on her shoulders and then running them up and down her bare arms. He bent his head so that their eyes could meet in the mirror's reflection. 'Constance, I promise you that this week I will put in the nomination and tell Phillip when he gets back.' His hands had gone round to her front and were massaging her through the bra, which he now slipped up over her breasts. 'No more talk about hints to others either for it would hurt Phillip's career very much and not be good for us either.'

Tom turned to Sarah and saw that the camera was already in action in following the scene at the dressing table of Judge Hopkins caressing and fondling the naked breasts of Constance Mason.

'Oh, what scope this would be for blackmail,' Sarah whispered to Tom. 'This should be a perfect film. Both faces very clear, what they are doing and more to the point, what they are saying.'

What the judge had said seemed to have appeased Constance for she got up and kissed him before going off into the bathroom while he undressed and after putting out the main light, got into bed. With the main cabin light off didn't make any difference to the filming for the infra red light was on and Constance now appeared in the doorway of the bathroom. She was wearing a filmy wisp of a nightdress that did not hide but just accentuated all that she had. Full ripe breasts, a trim waist, perfectly moulded thighs that held an abundance of pubic hair like a trimmed Van Dyke beard. She approached the bed shrugging of this film of material, and naked, knelt on the foot of it. The judge had only covered himself with the top sheet, and this, Constance slowly pulled down the bed. Down his chest and over his stomach till his erection sprang free and settled back onto his stomach. She bunched the sheet down round her knees and was squarely facing the camera when she spoke.

'You definitely promise to give Phillip the nomination?' When the judge nodded and said yes, she then moved forward and down onto her elbows either side of his legs and took hold of his prick, raised it upright and put the head of it into her mouth.

Sarah and Tom both looked at each and smiled. She saw that Tom had an erection from watching the couple on the bed so she moved round the camera and pressed up close behind him. Her hands went round to his fly and she deftly worked down the zip and pulled his hard member from out of his shorts. With one hand caressing his balls, she worked him fast with the other till he gasped and stiffened as his sperm shot out of his prick up against the wall.

While he wiped himself and put away his diminishing tool into his trousers, Sarah moved the camera slightly to catch a good sequence of the judge going down in between the legs of Constance with his tongue out as he pushed it into her bush that was in front of him. The follow up to this was of him moving up and entering her, his prick quite visible until it disappeared inside her.

Sarah suggested that they stop at this point for they had all they needed and there was no point in wasting film. Tom stopped the camera and she showed him the unloading process and then helped him stow away the equipment in a bag. With it safely deposited in his room, the film was taken into the improvised dark room where Sarah cut the film and developed the exposed section. Tom was disappointed when she held up some of the developed strips for him to see.

'You can't see much from that,' he complained.

'What do you mean?' she demanded. 'They're perfect. If this was run now through a projector onto the screen, it would be a wow.' When it was dry, she packed it into a small container that Tom had labelled with the two names of the people filmed along with the date and time. And so began to process of building up a library of many films that was to be their insurance against anyone of the people filmed making any trouble. Everybody was filmed twice, except those that were actually man and wife, though some were filmed more than this when they were having sex with a different person. The one most filmed was the Reverend Tyler, fucking nearly half of the male choir and about the same number of women from the Sunday Woman's Guild.

With their first film locked away in his cabin, Sarah kissed Tom and felt him start to rise up and so quickly undressed both him and herself and got onto the bed.

'Did you see the way he went down on her?' she asked as she stroked his cock and he stroked her breasts.

'Yes,' he replied, running his hand down over her stomach and pushed two fingers up inside her. This she liked for it was the first time he'd done this and she squirmed a little.

'Would you like to try it?'

'Now that's something I have done before,' he laughed and went on to tell her how, with his arms in plaster, he was able to suck on Caroline. She laughed at this and asked if he would like to do it again to which he said yes and so she moved for him to lie flat on the bed. She straddled his chest and he loved the sight of her above him, her tits well out in front and that lovely smile on her face and then looked to see her parted legs move up closer to him. The lips of her open sex came into view as she moved over him and she braced her hands on the wall and lowered herself down onto his waiting mouth. His hands, in use this time, held the cheeks of her bum as he began to lick and stick his tongue inside her.

She gave out many groans of pleasure as he licked and tickled her clit with his tongue in between sticking it up into her vagina. He was even able to nibble this clit though not properly when she was on top because it caused her to flinch and mash herself down when he did this. But he did enough to arouse her till she pleaded that enough was enough of that for she wanted his cock up inside her now.

She stayed on her knees and moved herself back down the bed till his cock was prodding her backside and she held it up so that she could lower herself down onto it. It was hot and throbbing and both gave out sighs as she sank down on it till she was sitting on his lap. They smiled at each other and his hands went up and caressed her tits as she began to move on him, bouncing herself up and down.

It didn't take long for her to bring her hands up to cover his and press her tits even harder as she moved faster on him and threw her head back and screamed out as she had her orgasm, triggering him to let go and flood her with his seed at the same time.

Her head fell forward, her hair spreading out wide like a fan over her shoulders as Tom could see the sweat rolling down between her breasts and feel their fluid seeping out of her and down between his thighs. It took several minutes before she had the strength to lift herself off of him and move further down the bed to take his still hard cock into her mouth to suck out any juices left inside him as well as suck off her own as she licked him clean.

They were both quite happy as they cuddled up afterwards to go off to sleep.

FRIDAY CAME and Mrs Towser, after finishing work, was told that she was being laid off which she didn't like but had to accept that Sarah would now be doing the cleaning and took the extra month's pay. So on the Saturday, she began to clean the cabins and Tom saw to the linen as usual. She was in cabin four, the brass one when Tom brought the linen in.

'Tom,' she said as she ran her hand up and down the golden phallic post at the end of the bed. 'Can I try this? With you naked on the bed watching me?' Her eyes were alight and she ran the tip of her tongue over her lips and Tom began to feel an erection coming and so agreed. She gave him a kiss and began to get undressed as he locked the cabin door before taking his own clothes off to prove that he wanted to see this with his cock really sticking out and throbbing.

He lay on the bed and marvelled at this beautiful woman who wanted to be with him all the time when she could really have had any number of men. She smiled at him from the bottom of the bed, running her hands up to those wonderful breasts before moving up close to the bed post and he saw the lips of her sex open as she moved one leg up and see the head of this brass cock move in between them. He saw that she didn't need to lubricate the post first for she was already wet in the anticipation of using this totem pole. The head disappeared and she let herself down, her eyes closed and her head thrown back as she went lower until the whole thing was inside her.

'Oh Tom,' she groaned, 'it's big but cold and it doesn't throb,' which didn't seem to stop her from moving herself up and down on this substitute. Both of her feet were planted on the floor and she was only bending and straightening her knees as she bounced on it, giving out little cries and moving faster as she neared her climax. Tom's cock was throbbing fit to burst but he kept his hands away for he knew she would want the real thing in a few minutes time.

Sweat began to form and run down her body as she moved and then gave out a muted gurgling scream as she orgasmed and her whole body shuddered as she came to a halt with her head hanging down on her chest.

'Oh my God,' she whispered as she lifted herself off, leaving the post smeared and glistening with her juices as she moved to the bed and fell on top of him. 'Hold and kiss me, Tom,' she moaned and feeling his throbbing cock squashed between them said, 'and then fuck me for you are better than that post and even though it was good, I'd rather have you inside me.' He held and kissed her for a minute or two before rolling her over so that he eased his cock as he moved on top of her.

'Tom. I do love you,' she whispered up at him as he lay on top of her. 'So much so that...that to prove it, will you take me like...like Professor Jenkins did.' Tom was just about to protest when he remembered that it was something that he shouldn't have known.

'How was that?' he asked.

'He...he fucked me up the rear. I didn't like it with him doing it, but...but it might be different with you.' Tom wanted to protest but she had said that she loved him that much that it was just another way of showing just how much and so he didn't say anything but rolled off of her.

'I haven't got any condoms here,' he said quietly.

'Don't use one. I want to feel you come inside me,' she said as she rolled over and got up onto her knees. Tom saw her breasts swing gently beneath her chest and loved this woman that was giving him the ultimate part of her body that he hadn't as yet stuck his prick into. 'Stick it in the usual place for lubrication first,' she said as he got in between her legs behind her and saw her wet vulva lower down and between the cheeks of her bum, the hole she wanted him to stick his cock in.

He didn't need to use his hand to guide his cock to the wet orifice there and it slipped in so easily and he pushed himself right up inside her knowing that he could never have reached as far as the bed post did. He moved himself several times inside, loving the soft pressure that surrounded his prick before pulling out but having to use his hand now to press it to the puckered flesh of her arsehole.

'Just relax now,' he said as he nuzzled the head of his cock there, smearing some of her juices around it and he felt her ease herself slightly and the he pushed forward, holding onto her hips to hold her steady. She gave out a gasp and he felt the inside muscle flex and try to prevent his entry but the head was well inside and from there, he slid in quite easily. By Christ, he thought as he felt his foreskin roll back, she's bloody tight. He too had to give out a gasp at just how tight it was compared to her vagina.

'Oh God, it's big,' she grunted out as he filled her backside, 'but I can feel the heat and it's throbbing. Now fuck me and let me feel you come.' So he began to move and really enjoyed the tightness as he fucked her up the arse and it wasn't long before he held her very tight and rammed himself hard up against her bum cheeks and came inside her. 'Wow, I can feel that,' she cried as he pumped himself dry before pulling out, her muscle still fighting as if to hold him there.

He was quickly off the bed and into the bathroom to wash himself and get his foreskin unrolled again but though he was slightly disgusted at what he'd just done, marvelled at how tight and different a fuck it was. Disgust took second place though to the pleasure he's gotten out of fucking such a confined aperture.

She was lying on her back with a smile on her face and her arms open wide for him when he returned to the bedroom.

'That's how much I love you, Tom,' she said as he slid into her arms for a kiss and have those big breasts squashed up against his chest. 'You don't hate me for asking you to do it that way?'

'Of course not, darling, for I love you too and will do anything to please you,' he said, returning her kisses and thought of himself as being the luckiest man on earth to have found such a woman as this.

They stayed in cabin four for another two hours and when he was ready again, he rolled over onto her and fucked her in the normal fashion. Over the next week they fucked in each cabin though not taking advantage of the equipment in cabins one and two for obvious reasons. She did rather like cabin seven with the mirrors and this was the one they used the most and both had the enjoyment of watching what they did to each other.

As it was now a Saturday, Tom had to gently remind her that the office was used for the weekly card game and that the photo equipment had to be removed from the kitchen. She kept silent about what had happened before in there and took the stuff out into Tom's cabin. He didn't go viewing them that evening so didn't know if they had another girl in there or not. Instead, the camera was set up in the locker for cabin two. This was the one used for the film shows and had the rack installed in its own cupboard on the wall. It had been booked over the phone and wondered where the woman, who phoned, had got to hear about it and specifically asked for this one.

It was vacant and so he agreed to let it and was still a bit uneasy when the woman arrived to book in while her husband, question mark, stayed out in the car. Usually cabins one to seven went to regular customers that he knew, not strangers but sensed that she was not of any law enforcement agency but had decided to film them just in case.

He could see later, after they had moved in that they were genuine and nothing to do with the law for she knew exactly how to remove the panels that covered the bottom of the bed when it was in its upright position. These taken away revealed the webbing straps that crossed the frame instead of a mattress. Sarah was in the locker with him working the camera and watched as the man undressed and lay down on the webbing, settling himself down so that his cock and balls would hang through the webbing. His wife, it was assumed, put the ankle belts onto him and then fixed his wrists into the straps that were attached to the small pulley wheel at the top of the rack.

The fittings for these wrist straps had been specifically made so that though there was a certain amount of tension when the wheel was turned, it wasn't enough to actually dislocate the shoulders for the retaining pins would come out if over used. There was enough tension in the wrist restraints to prevent whoever was tied to them from moving which was what it was all about.

Well, the naked man was fixed to the rack and the wheel turned to hold him tight and in place before the woman undressed and paraded about for him to see her body, which wasn't that good by the normal criteria. Above the rack in the cupboard was a variety of whips and canes and she had selected a thin cane and was now holding it in her hand and as she moved from one side of the rack to the other, if he didn't move his head quick enough, got slashed with the cane across his bare bum. She was also talking the whole time as she moved about, giving him questions and if he gave the wrong answer, another crack across the arse with the cane.

'What's this between my legs?' was one question.

'Pussy!' Crack, and another red weal appeared on his backside. 'Cunt!' Crack. 'Fanny?' Crack. 'Vagina?' and you could see his body tense up but no whack with the cane this time as she moved round the rack again.

'What are these?' she asked, pointed to her breasts. Tom and Sarah were now playing this game too, giving out their answers but not getting the cane when they got it wrong. The man took six blows before he said 'Orbs,' and missed out on another slash.

His backside was fast becoming quite red and it wasn't until it started to bleed did he cry out enough. The woman then threw a cushion from the chair onto the floor and pushed it under the bed and went down herself and stretched out on her back as she slid under the rack. The camera couldn't catch what she did but it was obvious that she was there underneath sucking him off.

He was then, after she had finished underneath the rack, released and it was her turn now to be racked though face upwards this time. Now it was his turn to strut round, his backside really red in colour, and he carried a small three-thong whip that he stroked over her body asking her similar questions and getting flicked across her stomach and breasts with every wrong answer.

He finished up by going between her legs and sucking and chewing her out until she had her orgasm.

'Well, it takes all sorts,' Sarah said as they watched him trying to get his whole face up inside her. 'That is one game we're definitely not playing,' and Tom had to agree with her on this but it was another film piece to add to their archives.

They went to church the next morning with it being Sunday and heard the story of how Samson was betrayed by Delilah and Tom whispered to Sarah that they should set the camera up in cabin seven for Tyler would be taking a woman in there that afternoon. He was right and surprised to see that it was Shirley Rivers, the wife of the sheriff.

'Now this definitely is insurance,' said Tom as Shirley Rivers stretched out naked on Tyler's altar (the bed) to receive the blessing of the Lord (his cock) as he climbed on and fucked her. To wash away any sin, Tyler's words, she had to go down and suck on his wet prick and lick him clean.

'It can't get any better than that,' Sarah breathed as she watched the woman perform fellatio on the Reverend.

'It can,' Tom assured her. 'Wait until he's fucking one of the young men.'

As already mentioned, the Right Reverend Tyler became the most filmed man of their archives along with nearly all of the most notable people of the town over the next six months.

During this period Tom took the bull by the horns and asked Sarah if she would marry him, to which she said yes and so two months later they were wed. Tom had also had an ulterior motive in asking her, even though he loved her as life itself, with her being married to him, she couldn't testify against him if anything ever went wrong in respect of the activities that went on in the motel. Not that she had or even thought about anything like this, she married him because of love.

WELL, THERE'S not much that really could be said about Tom and his predilection for watching other people having sex for one would only be repeating oneself, but there is a little bit more about what happened in later years.

After three years of marriage and sex as often as Tom could manage it, Sarah announced that she would like to have a child, or more than one. Tom agreed to this and she stopped taking the pill and a year later, she gave birth to a son who they christened William after her father.

As much as Tom loved being a father to his beautiful wife, he found the motel room they lived in now too cramped for the three of them and it was when she announced that she was pregnant again that he decided to do something about it. He didn't tell Sarah of his plans but made sure that his insurance on the motel was up to date and they had a rain storm and a good north wind blowing when he set fire to the woods to the north of the motel.

He was quickly back to the motel to tell Sarah that the woods were on fire and to get the baby and the film archives out into the pick-up. He also made sure that the residue of the bank robbery money was safe as he drove the pick-up out onto the highway and then woke everybody up who was staying at the motel and got them to leave before he rang the local fire station to tell them of the encroaching fire.

Then it was all chaos for the rest of the night. Guests streaming out and fire engines trying to get through to halt the advancing fire. Bulldozers were brought up from town and the fire chief told Tom that he didn't think that they would be able to halt the fire before it reached the motel for it was more important for him to prevent it reaching the petrol station. So the bulldozers were put to work to try and create a fire break between Tom's property and this gas station while the fire-fighters tried to keep the fire in check.

With all the guests evacuated from the motel, Tom agreed that the gas station had to be saved first and so watched them clear the ground between the motel and it and though the firemen did their best, they couldn't save the motel from going up in flames.

But to the town's relief, they managed to clear a space wider than the fire could jump, spending hours spraying this cleared ground as they watched Love Motel burn to the ground, not counting the other houses that were on the north eastern side of the motel on Elm Street. The rain helped them a little to save the station and it was this that partly raised the reason for the fire in the first place.

Sarah cried as she watched what had been her home get consumed by the flames but Tom held her tight and assured her that the motel, like the phoenix, would rise from the ashes. It was three days before the fire chief could look over the ground where the fire had started and in his report stated that a tree had been struck by lightning during the storm. Tom smiled at this for he had started the fire at the very tree that had been struck many years ago that had caused the fire that had killed his parents.

So it was entered and the insurance companies had to pay out. Tom got back the value of the property destroyed and also claimed and even went to court and won for his claim of loss of revenue that the motel generated until such time that a new one could be built. He'd taken his register and accounts to substantiate his claim of earnings for the books showed that he was fully booked every night and it would be in the insurance company's interests to pay up quickly so that he could rebuild.

The court, held in town, supported Tom and the company had to pay up but they insisted that with the new motel that it be built of concrete and such and not of wood. To this Tom agreed for it had been his intention to do so anyway for he had new ideas that he wanted to put into place.

He traded in his pick-up and bought another camper van, big enough for the three, soon to be four, until he could sit down with an architect and design a new motel to take the place of the old one. Sarah was thankful that he had warned her in time for she managed to salvage all their clothes and personal things as well as all the records and films they had collected.

The new motel he designed was to be an open square again but joined up and of two stories, eight rooms per floor per side and constructed of brick and cement but without the viewing lockers this time. For he had other ideas instead what with the new technology that had been brought onto the market.

The office would be where the original had been but above this would be their living quarters and they would have another section up on top which would be three bedrooms. This top section would have crenellated stone to make it look like the top of a fort. This whole section would be connected by an internal staircase for their inside access. So as to give the place a balanced look, another room would be constructed on the other side with these same battlements, though the large room itself would be used for storage.

The motel would then have forty six rooms to let, sixteen of these, the back section, would be made over as fun rooms as before though dispensing with the rack this time. Six being mirrored for this seemed the most popular and two each of the others.

For Tom and Sarah's living quarters, as said, the top part was divided into three bedrooms, theirs and one each for the children though the second was still yet to be born as she was still carrying. The one below was their lounge and kitchen cum dining area while the ground floor would be the office, small, for at the back would be the dark room and a television monitoring section. This was because each room of the motel, except their quarters, would have a camera installed. This would be linked up to a television in each room. Though unbeknown to any occupants, they would also be linked up to the monitor room behind the office desk. In there would be six small sets so that six rooms could be viewed at the same time and if there was anything worth recording, it could be done.

Due to a sign in the office which told guests that they could video their stay at the motel caused many of them to buy the small thirty minute cassettes and even get Tom to make copies so that they could have one each. Every time someone asked about this, Tom would go with them to their room and explain that all they had to do was switch the camera on with the cassette in the recorder beneath the television set also turned on.

He said then all they had to do was stand in front of the camera and give their names and do whatever they wanted to do. Afterwards, they could rewind the video and watch themselves on the television set. If they didn't like what they saw, they could do it all over again or destroy the video if they wished.

It was surprising the number of people who signed false names in the register when booking in and yet gave their proper names when they wanted to tape themselves. This built up another library for Tom and Sarah for down in his monitor room, a console would light up with the room number whenever the camera was switched on and so Tom or Sarah could make their own copy of what went on and so he was really back into the viewing mode again but without having to leave the office.

MRS TOWSER was only too glad to be taken on again as a cleaner and even had another young woman to help her this time when the motel had opened for it was too much for her to cope on her own. With more than double the number of rooms, they still were able to more than half fill the motel every night.

Sarah went into labour and produced a daughter that they named Lillian after her mother. Tom was delighted with his new child and happy that they would very soon be having sex again as before. He marvelled at how she was still able to have her body return to its previous delightful looking self. Her tummy now flat and able to have him lay on top of her as they fucked and suck on her breasts which were now even bigger. Though he didn't really like the milk that they produced which was really only for the baby but would still have that twinge of jealousy when the baby was sucking there.

With cleaners at the motel, Sarah was quite happy to look after the children and take turns at watching and taping the sexual antics of other couples in the rooms. She and Tom would then copy some of them, especially if they did something quite different though these sightings were becoming very rare now for they'd seen most of what other people could manage.

So Tom still got his thrill of watching these other people having sex and was now able to do the same and have a wonderful woman to do it with, and did so for many of the years left for them to enjoy doing so.

THE END

Here is a sample from another story you may enjoy:

Amy Redek

UP FOR SALE

AUCTIONED TO THE HIGHEST BIDDER!

Hot Gay Erotica

"Young male, twenty-three and of good health and fit is being put up for auction for a period of six months to do exactly all that you order. This auction begins as of now for five days and he will go to the highest bidder that goes above the starting price of two thousand dollars."

I was sweating when I pressed the send key and hoped that I would somehow get somebody to pay me a good sum to be what really boils down to being their slave for six months. I think I lost at least six pounds of weight with my sweating out those five days until the time came round to find out if anyone at least made a decent offer. I contacted Ebay to get the answer and was told that the bidding went through over twenty people and the final offer was eight thousand, five hundred dollars. Was that acceptable?

Christ! Did that give me a hard on or not? I couldn't help but jerk myself off right there and then as I looked at the figure again, and it wasn't long after shooting my load that I replied that I accepted this offer and by return, was given the name and address of the person that had made this enormous bid.

I was somewhat dismayed that it wasn't some wealthy woman on finding out that it was a man that made this offer, guessing that I was about to enter the world of homosexuality. But beggars cannot be choosers, though on reflection, it was a form of prostitution that I was offering and I was now committed. Though even if the money had been transferred to my account, I could still pay it back if I didn't like the man who paid that amount. But on reflection realised that I would still have to pay PayPal their fee and probably more to the person who had made the offer, which in my present financial state, couldn't.

After an almost sleepless night, weighing up the pros and cons of what I was doing, selling myself and my soul, decided to burn my boats. I got up and packed what little I had into one suitcase and took it to the station and put it into storage there. I also wrote a short note to my landlord saying that I was leaving the flat and put the keys with the note into an envelope and sealed it for posting. Having made my decision and on returning to the flat, I finally got off to sleep, not having to worry about what else was in the flat because I had rented it furnished.

So the next morning, after making sure I really cleaned myself in the shower and getting properly dressed, went off to the address I had been given, posting the letter on the way. I had to travel on a bus for this was on the other side of town in what I called the posh part, for the houses there were rather expensive and only really for the elite.

On leaving the bus, I had to ask two different people for directions to the boulevard that I wanted. This part of town didn't have street names as they were either boulevards or avenues, they were that posh. I found the one I wanted and soon stood outside the address I had been given to see a veritable mansion. Now this was way out of my sphere and it was with some trepidation that I walked up the gravelled drive that curved round an elaborate fountain and up the few steps to the entrance that stood between two massive pillars. My finger wavered as I pressed the bell button by the side and waited.

A pert young woman dressed as a maid answered the door and looked at me. 'Yes?' she enquired of me.

'Er, my name is Mark Trent and I have an appointment with Mr. Branson,' I said.

No, it wasn't the Branson of Virgin fame, or related, but another whose Christian name was Dennis. I was the virgin, without fame.

'Oh, yes. You are expected,' she said with a shy smile. 'Please enter and I will inform the master that you have arrived.' She stood aside for me to enter a very large entrance hall that had a huge circular dome made of glass to give ample light to the area. A huge staircase on my left wound round and up to the next floor where there were two doors either side of what looked like a corridor or hallway going back into the building. Facing me were three doors on this ground floor and I heard the door close behind me and she came past me, saying that I was to follow her.

We went through the door on the right into a short corridor with a door at the far end and one to the left, which she stopped at and knocked. A voice was heard with the word 'Enter' and she opened the door to announce me.

'Mr. Trent sir,' she said, and beckoned me to step forward. I entered what looked like the master's study and saw the man himself, just putting a book back on a much crowded shelf. In fact there were many shelves packed with books. He looked to be about forty years of age, about the same height as me, that being nearly six foot and looked quite fit without any sign of a paunch. His hair was black with a slight tinge of grey at the sides. He had blue eyes and a lovely smile as he looked at me.

'Sarah. Mr. Trent, his first name being Mark, is now a member of the household for the next six months. Though I expect you to see that he learns the house rules and is, when I am not at home, expected to follow whatever things you need to be done in keeping this house in good order. Though when I am at home, he is to be treated as a guest to follow my orders, which as you will find out, will be variable. Any questions?'

'Well only one sir. What room will he be sleeping in?' she said.

'Mine.'

'Oh,' was all she could say to that and gave me a strange look.

I think that my face had gone quite red at the blatant way he had answered her question, and was somewhat relieved when he asked me to follow him.

We followed Sarah out of the room through another door and as she turned to the right, we turned to the left and went up a short staircase onto the next landing and went along to the end to go into the last room.

This turned out to be his bedroom, well with seeing a large bed on one side of the pair of windows, it was the only thing that came to mind.

He had ushered me inside and closed the door behind him and walked over to a cabinet that I could see held quite a variety of bottles and glasses.

'I'm only doing this once, Mark,' he said as he opened the cabinet and took out two glasses and poured out some drink into them and then passed a glass over to me. 'From now on, when we enter this room, you will pour out our drinks and see to the cleaning of them later to be returned into the cabinet.'

'Yes sir,' I replied, taking the proffered glass and had him clink the pair together.

'Cheers,' he said before taking a big gulp of his drink. 'Now you are here to see to my every need and some others that might crop up.' This last he said with something of a snigger in his smile. 'Have you ever had male sex before?' he asked, taking a smaller sip of his glass this time.

I nearly choked on my drink at the question.

'N-no sir,' I replied, realising what I had let myself in for.

'A tyro? Well it might work,' he replied, finishing off his drink and offering the empty glass to me. Knowing my place, I took it from him and placed it on the open cabinet and quickly finished mine to put there also before turning round.

'Well let's start you on your education of this, for that is why I made that offer for you. To be my bed mate and all that goes along with it. The first being that I want you to suck on my cock.' I had by now guessed that this would happen and wished that I had never offered myself through the internet.

He moved over to the bed and sat down on the edge and pointed to the floor between his open legs. What the fuck have you done, a voice in my mind cried out. I closed my mind to this question and moved over to where he was sitting and, trembling, went down onto my knees and on placing my hands on his knees, looked up at him.

'Well? Get my prick out of my trousers and suck me off,' he said.

So, with fluttering hands, I pulled down the zip of his trousers and put my hand inside to find that he was wearing pants and could feel that his cock was hard inside. I fumbled at pulling down the pants and actually, for the first time, took hold of a hard cock that wasn't mine. I had quite often jerked myself off in the past, but this was the first time that I had my hand on somebody else's.

I managed to get his erection out of his pants, also pulling his balls out at the same time until his cock was now in full view in front of me. I was mesmerised like a rabbit in front of a venomous snake, holding his throbbing cock in my hand as I looked at the red and purple head that was showing itself with his foreskin halfway down it.

'The idea Mark, is that you take the head into your mouth and suck on it and also use your tongue over the flesh as you use your hand to rub up and down on the shaft.'

This snapped me awake and with some trepidation, bent forward and for the first time, took another man's cock into my mouth. It felt quite hot and it was almost like a large piece of rubber, for it moved in that fashion as I pushed the head round in my mouth as I sucked on it. I was also using my hand to rub that soft skin that moved so easily up and down the shaft of this cock that I had in my mouth.

Bloody hell, I said to myself. Sucking on another man's cock. Am I doing it right? Well he'll tell you if you're not, the voice in my head told me. What happens when he cums? Do I spit it out or swallow it?

He answered that unspoken question, his hand now on my head and gently pulling it onto his cock. 'When I cum, you are expected to swallow it and to keep on sucking until I pull out. Make sure that the head is clean first.'

I was nodding my head but not in answer to his order. For it was his hand that was making it nod as he kept pulling my head onto his cock and I then gripped his cock more firmly in my hand so that he wouldn't choke me by pushing his cock too far into my mouth.

I must have been doing it right, sucking and running my tongue round the bare flesh of the head for he didn't say anything otherwise. So with my eyes looking at the bush of hair at his groin, I kept sucking on him and felt the head start to expand and then nearly choked on the first shot of his cum hitting the back of my throat. I almost gagged and managed to close my gullet before that next shot of cum joined the first lot. Still more came pumping into my mouth, actually feeling it coming up along the underside of his cock, till it stopped with me now having a mouthful of his cum.

Now I had never even tasted what my own cum was like when I had jerked myself off, so this was a first. I closed my eyes and took a deep breath as I opened my gullet and swallowed his cum. It slid down my throat like a raw egg and only then did my tongue really get a taste of it. Slightly salty but otherwise, not too bad.

For some reason, I felt quite proud of myself…

If you enjoyed this sample then look for **Up for Sale.**

Also by this Author

The Painted Sword

Cruise Control

Wild Pleasures

Lending My Beloved

Lady of Cuckolds

Lady of Pleasure

Lady Magenta

Sexually Overdosed

Meeting My Fancy Dear

Prison Sex Slave

Chasing A Shadow

The Hostel

The Island

Thirst for Drugs and Pleasure

Forgotten Identity

Grey Memories

Chronos: Time Machine

The Hard Bomber

Honeymoon Abduction

The Yacht Sins

Summer at the Villa

Practice Makes Perfect

Stranger Danger

Following Father's Footsteps

The Square Circle

The Wizard of Kos

Out in the Real World

Me, Carol and Raoul

About the Author

George Eliot was a famous writer, though at the time, only male authors were recognised. It was in fact the pen name of Mary Ann Evans, a female.

When I started writing, I thought that if a woman could use a male name, why, with me being male, why couldn't I use the name of a female? Though to be different, I made my writer's name from an anagram of my real name.

I wasn't the brightest spark in my school days and it was only while being in the Merchant Navy did I self-educate myself. That being mostly literature, classical music and artists, like Tolstoy, Chopin and Rembrandt. After leaving the navy, I had several jobs, finishing up by being a working boss using my own maxim that 'Management is the art of delegation.'

It's when I became self-employed that I began to write, though sadly, not many of my books can be published because of certain laws that forbid certain aspects of life. This never fazed me for I was really writing just to please myself having a wide range of the human psych.

Having written ninety stories, my only aim now is to reach one hundred. I give thanks to the publishers for at least putting some of my efforts out for others to enjoy as much as I did in the writing of them.

From the Author

Check my page on Amazon and my blog for Updates and interesting info.

Author Central – http://www.amazon.com/Amy-Redek/e/B00A48NQ72
Author Blog – http://amy-redek.awesomeauthors.org/

If you enjoyed any of my books then please share the love and click like on my books in Amazon.

If you write me a review and send me an email I will send you a free book, or many.
(Just know that these emails are filtered by my publisher.)

Good news is always welcome.

One Last Thing, For Kindle Readers...

When you turn the page, Kindle will give you the opportunity to rate this book and share your thoughts on Facebook and Twitter. If you enjoyed my writings, would you please take a few seconds to let your friends know about it? Because... when they enjoy they will be grateful to you and so will I.

Thank You!

Amy Redek
amy_redek@awesomeauthors.org